FOR THE LOVE
OF MURPHY

FOR THE LOVE OF MURPHY

•

CJ Love

AVALON BOOKS
NEW YORK

Published by Thomas Bouregy & Co., Inc.
160 Madison Avenue, New York, NY 10016

Library of Congress Cataloging-in-Publication Data

Love, C J.
    For the love of Murphy / CJ Love.
        p.   cm.
    ISBN 978-0-8034-9966-9 (hardcover : acid-free paper)
    I. Title.

PS3612.O83385F67   2009
813'.6—dc22

                                    2009004068

PRINTED IN THE UNITED STATES OF AMERICA
ON ACID-FREE PAPER
BY HADDON CRAFTSMEN, BLOOMSBURG, PENNSYLVANIA

With love to my daughter, Mary, my first fan.

Chapter One

The storm intensified. Trees bent with the force of the wind and explosions of thunder cracked overhead. Lightning split open the sky. In the flash of brightness, Sheriff Wade Murphy saw a pair of boots sticking out from behind an oak tree. He inched forward but there was no need for caution. The boots belonged to a dead man. It was a gruesome sight—the man lay spread-eagle with the whole front of him torn open. Bits of flesh clung to the snaps of his shredded vest. His blank eyes stared skyward and the rain fell into them.

Murphy turned away to study the immediate area, the thicket, and the mud. He walked toward another tree and there he saw what he searched for: a small boot print that spilled over with rain.

He tracked the prints a quarter mile before he saw movement to his left. "Katie Thomas!" he shouted.

The young woman ran.

Murphy bolted after her. The rain teemed and slashed sideways through the trees. Thunder exploded. The girl stumbled and Murphy caught her. Pulling her to her feet, he hollered over the storm, "I am Sheriff Murphy. I am going to help you."

She took a step backward, lifted a pistol, and aimed it straight at Murphy's face.

"Hold up," he said, raising his hands and watching her trigger finger. "Did you hear me? I'm Sheriff Murphy. Your brother Todd asked me to find you. Todd's at the stagecoach doctoring Ben Raines."

She looked wild with her long hair matted against her cheeks. Blood covered the front of her dress and it had splattered onto her arms and neck.

Her thumb cocked the weapon.

Murphy raised his forearm just as the girl squeezed off a shot. A bullet sizzled past his face. He brought his right hand up and knocked the weapon from her grip. The gun sailed upward as another stroke of lightning split the sky. Murphy saw Katie Thomas clearly in that moment. He thought she would be scared, but she didn't look scared; she looked determined, murderously so, and when she saw where the pistol landed she lunged for it.

Enraged, Murphy leaped after her.

She missed the weapon by an arm's length and then crawled toward it.

Murphy got one hand on the band of her skirt. He yanked hard, pulling her backward.

She shrieked, twisted around, and fought him like a wildcat. Murphy grabbed her shoulders and pushed her backward, but suddenly his force was unnecessary. Katie Thomas had fainted in the mud.

Nathan Bates had been shot dead while searching for survivors of the stagecoach robbery. Murphy felt a stab of guilt. What he had been most grieved over was that Bates had been assigned to take his place as sheriff of Victor City. Now Murphy would remain sheriff until Logan County sent another replacement for him.

God, forgive my selfishness, he had prayed, but Murphy could not shake his disappointment until he had to tell Foster Garrett's parents that their nineteen-year-old son had been shot in the head during the stage robbery. That put things right in Murphy's mind, watching Mattie Garrett in the throws of hysteria over the death of her oldest child.

He contacted two more families that day with the same news while Dr. Todd Thomas treated the two survivors. One man, Darryl Jones, remained missing and Murphy called on five local men to search for him. The man Murphy found dead behind the old oak had no identification on him, which was not unusual, but it made it difficult to trace family members to inform them of the death. Murphy wired the Lincoln depot for the names of all the travelers on the stage.

Then there was the matter of Katie Thomas.

There was one thing Murphy prided himself on and that was his ability to read human behavior. Maybe it was a result of being the interim sheriff for the past five years, but Murphy had never been wrong after his first impression left him wary of someone's intentions. Todd claimed his sister was beautiful, vibrant, and sweet-spirited. Maybe Murphy was narrow-minded, but he'd never met a sweet-spirited woman yet who toted a snub nose five-shot and tried to kill the local lawman.

Now, a good argument was that Katie Thomas was frightened, startled, and all out of sorts the day of the robbery. Maybe she hadn't heard Murphy say that he was the sheriff; maybe she didn't hear him explain that Todd waited for her at the stage. Maybe. But his intuition told him differently. Katie Thomas knew what she was doing in the woods after the stage holdup and she knew how to use the pistol, for she wielded it with great proficiency. No, Murphy believed Katie Thomas was trouble and he knew precisely how this story would end.

"Is she awake?" Murphy asked, coming into the doctor's house through the back door. It was the second day he asked the same question.

Todd stood at the table preparing lunch. "She's still in bed." He did not act defensively to Murphy's inquiries for he seemed to understand that, as sheriff, Murphy needed to set records in order regarding the stage holdup. But neither did Todd act as though he wanted Murphy to interrogate his sister. He was protective over her ever since Murphy delivered her to him unconscious and covered in blood.

The first time Murphy had met Todd was on the stage from Denver to Victor City. They both had been eager to start new lives. Murphy planned to act as sheriff only long enough to save money to buy the property he had his eye on south of Victor City. Todd, on the other hand, had no other dream but to heal the sick and mend the broken. If he was not with a patient then he studied plant roots or mixed concoctions to ease pain and clear infection. It was a rare sight to see the young doctor without a medical tome beneath his nose.

Todd paused from slicing bread. "I realized last night that I never thanked you for finding Katie."

"Forget it."

"I will not forget it. You put your plans on hold for me. You should be in Denver right now collecting two colts."

Murphy stepped farther into the room and leaned on the cold box. "I canceled the order."

"Maybe it won't take so long for Logan County to send a replacement."

"Let's hope it's less than three years this time. How's Ben Raines doing this morning?"

"He's out again. That's why I thought to come and eat lunch. The pain medication I gave him will keep him out for a time." He set the knife aside and pulled two silver pieces out of his pocket. "Here are the slugs I dug out of his shoulder and side. You said you wanted them."

Murphy pushed off the cold box and took the bullets from Todd. "Has he said anything that makes sense yet?"

"He mostly groans in pain but at least I get water into him when he wakes. I saw that one of the wounds is infected now." Todd picked up the knife again to slice off a chunk of ham. "Ben is strong and he's fighting, but I'd say his chances of surviving this are slim."

Murphy had known Ben Raines for a long time and it made him sick to know a fine man lay dying upstairs because of someone's greed and murderous intentions. "I would like to talk to Katie. Will you ask her to come downstairs?"

"I spoke to her this morning. She doesn't remember what happened."

"What do you mean?"

He had not meant to sound harsh but Todd paused to look at Murphy. "I told her that we searched for her when the stage was late and that you found her wandering in the woods with blood splattered all over the front of her dress."

"And what did she say?"

"Not much." He transferred his food to a plate. "She started to cry and swore she didn't hear gunshots or remember running through the woods." He laid waxed paper over the cold meat and cleaned the knife with a cloth. "Katie has had a shock, Murphy. Her mind is trying to protect her."

"Protect her? You think she has amnesia?"

Todd nodded, looking pleased that Murphy had heard of the condition. "To be precise, I believe she has anterograde amnesia. It refers to the total, or in Katie's case, partial loss of memory caused by a brain injury. She hit her head when the stage tipped. It's as simple as that."

"Simple? It doesn't explain all the dead people scattered through the woods."

Todd took a bite of food and smirked at Murphy. "Well, that's your job, isn't it? I'm healing the wounded."

"Listen, Doctor, until Ben Raines wakes, your sister is

the only one who can explain what happened out there. I want to talk to her."

Todd lowered the food in his hand. "She has been through a traumatic experience. I hope you'll be patient with her. Katie needs time to mend."

"I'm a patient man," Murphy reminded him, taking the bread from Todd's hand. He moved toward the back door. "I'll wait another day to talk to her." He took a bite of the food and stepped out of the house.

Katie chose the periwinkle-colored dress with a white lace collar, wasp waist, and leg-of-mutton sleeves. Sore from head to foot, she had been scratched, beaten, and bruised . . . but at least she was fashionable.

She studied her reflection in the full-length mirror. Her usually smooth complexion looked a pale backdrop to the blotchy marks across her cheeks. Finding a brush, she sat on the edge of the bed to untangle her hair.

Katie was so happy to be with Todd again. It had been six years since she saw him last. She had only been a young girl when Todd went off to Denver to attend medical school. They had seen each other during term breaks but when he accepted the post in Victor City, they kept in touch by telegraph and by letter.

But she dreaded going downstairs. Todd would start all over again. Ever since she awoke yesterday, he had nagged her with the same questions: *Did you see who stopped the stage? Did you and another passenger run from the scene together? Who was he? Do you know his name?* Katie did not know she had been in a stage, let alone why she had run from it or whether someone had run with her. Her memory was unclear. She had a vague feeling of unease and not because Todd had told her that she had been in a stagecoach accident. It was something else, something with white light and blood . . .

Katie got to her feet. Maybe she didn't want to know. Whatever it was shortened her breath. She heard her heart beating in her ears. If she remembered what happened, then it would be real . . . She walked out of the bedroom and onto the landing.

Todd used his home as his office. Brick-red wallpaper with gold stripping garnished the walls in the front room. Beneath the chair railing, shelves were crammed with texts and medical tomes. Red flowered draperies covered the windows and gold twisted rope tied them back.

Katie stepped off the stairs to face three doors on her left. She found Todd when she opened the second door. He stood in the center of the room and when he saw her, he introduced her to Mrs. Crowe, to her daughter, Sarah, and to her son, Barney. Katie nodded in greeting to all three and then sat in a chair by the door.

"What's the matter, Katie?" Todd asked while he examined Sarah. "Done too much? I told you to stay in bed."

"You shouldn't scorn the nearly dead."

The little girl lay back on the table. "Am I going to die?"

Todd frowned at Katie while touching the child's stomach and side. Behind glasses, his blue eyes narrowed, and his blond hair fell over his brow. "Thank you for bringing up the subject." He smiled at his patient. "By the feel of things, young lady, you've a broken rib."

Barney watched them from his spot in the corner of the room. He appeared to be about ten years old and his shaggy brown hair stuck up in the back. Dirt smudged his jaw. "Is Sarah going to be all right, Dr. Todd?"

"She will be when you stop trying to convince her that she can ride a pig like you ride a pony." He moved toward a cabinet to remove a long white bandage.

"It is possible to ride a pig," Katie explained to the boy. "Dr. Todd did it himself once when he fell backward over our paddock fence." She saw her brother's stern features in her peripheral vision. "He held on by the ears, I believe." Katie smiled at Barney. "I declare he rode it all the way across the yard. I nearly went deaf from all his swearing . . ."

Barney giggled but Mrs. Crowe let out an "Oh my," staring at the doctor.

"*Swearing* . . . that he would never ride a pig again because it cannot and should not be done." She shrugged an apology at Todd.

"I bet you're hungry, aren't you Katie?" Todd asked irritably, pulling money from his pant pocket. "There's a kitchen across the road."

Katie stood and took the money he offered. Barney still stared at her and she asked, "Will you show me the way, Barney, if it is all right with your mother, of course."

Sitting in a rocker on the front porch of his office, Murphy saw Barney and Katie step off the walkway in front of Todd's office. He watched them for a moment before getting to his feet. Katie Thomas moved with simple grace. Two fellows in the street hesitated from work and took off their hats to gaze at her. Few men would resist staring at such a beauty with her long pale hair and blue eyes. She resembled a china doll, Murphy thought, for she looked fragile and demure. But then, he had seen a different side of her. Stepping off the porch, he tossed away the pick he had been chewing, adjusted his hat, and followed them.

Being a gentleman, Barney opened doors for Katie and held her hand when she stepped over a threshold. They entered Marigold's Kitchen and sat in the clean and neat dining room. Barney held the chair for her and Katie complimented him on his good manners. "You look hurt," he said, explaining his behavior.

They ordered thick slices of ham and eggs with glasses of milk. "What do you do for fun, Barney?" she asked when he set his glass on the table.

"I like to fish and hunt. I want to be a fur trapper when I grow up."

She nodded. "I like the mountains and living off the land. Maybe I should be a fur trapper too."

Barney giggled.

"What's tickling your funny bone?" someone asked, standing next to Barney's chair.

Katie gazed at the man wearing dark trousers and a black suede jacket. He was tall, lean, and broad-shouldered. He held a wide-brimmed hat in his hand.

"Hey ya, Sheriff. Miss Thomas wants to be a fur trapper like me."

So this was Murphy, Sheriff Wade Murphy, the man Todd had told her so much about in his letters. His strait brow rose as he studied her with his gray-blue eyes. He had an angular jaw with a new growth of beard and mustache that looked as though he had not shaved that morning. His rich brown hair fell in waves on either side of his face and it curled at the jacket collar. He took the seat next to Barney and said, "You can't be a trapper."

"Why not?" she tried to sound wounded by his words.

Barney giggled again. "Because trappers spit and cuss and they never take baths."

"No baths?" she asked, leaning forward. "I see the attraction. When do we start?"

Murphy and the boy peered at each other as if they could not believe Katie wasn't fond of perfumed baths. Barney said politely, "I think we should wait. You couldn't walk across the street this morning without my help."

"Yes, but thanks to you I'm feeling much better."

"My mother said you can't remember what happened to you."

The sheriff poked Barney in the ribs while keeping a serene look on his face.

Katie pushed at the plate in front of her. She didn't want Barney to feel badly about what he'd blurted out, so she clarified, "I think my harrowing experience confirms that I'd make an excellent trapper, don't you?" She gazed at the sheriff. "I mean, it proves that I'm somewhat practiced in survival."

The sheriff grimaced comically. "It does not." He winked at Barney. "It only proves that you're somewhat clumsy." Then something out the window caught his attention. "Barney, your mother is looking for you."

Her eyes followed the direction Murphy pointed to and Katie recognized Mrs. Crowe on the walk outside. Katie waved at Sarah, who appeared heartier than she had in the examining room.

Barney said, "Good-bye, Miss Katie. Thank you for breakfast. See you, Sheriff."

"You've made a fast friend," Murphy observed, watching the boy leave the restaurant.

Katie smiled at the sheriff, liking him. She hadn't met him and felt awkward for a moment. For the last year, Todd the Matchmaker had asked Katie to visit Victor City so that she could meet Wade Murphy, claiming that he was a good man with a generous heart. "I'm Katie Thomas."

"I know," he replied, offering nothing in return. He appeared content to sit and count the scratches on her face.

"Everyone calls you Murphy, isn't that right, or Wade?"

"Sheriff Murphy."

"Sheriff," she repeated. "My brother told me that you saved my life. Thank you."

"I didn't save your life."

She stopped smoothing the napkin in her lap. "You didn't?"

"I saved my life."

"Oh." She placed the napkin on the table. "Todd told me—"

"I did my job, Miss Thomas." He did not act the least bit friendly. He held his jaw rigidly and his brows drew close together. "Tell me what happened three days ago."

His tone caused her stomach to flutter and Katie sat straighter. She hesitated only because she didn't know what to say. Murphy didn't seem to be the type of man who would let her alone if she felt strained or disquieted.

"I asked you a question."

"I don't . . . I don't remember anything."

"Then tell me the last thing you do remember."

"I . . . woke yesterday."

"Before that," he said sharply. "What's the last thing you remember?"

Katie stared out the window, thinking hard. "I said good-bye to my aunt and cousin."

"At the depot?"

"No . . ." She glanced at the sheriff again. "Yes, *they* were leaving for New York. My aunt asked me if I was certain I didn't want to go with them. Obviously I didn't want to go to New York . . ."

"Why not?"

Katie didn't want to tell the sheriff why she didn't want to go to New York. "Because I wanted to come and visit Todd."

She saw it in his posture that he didn't believe her. He took the fork off Barney's plate and twirled it with his fingers. "What day did your aunt leave for New York?"

"August fifteenth."

"So you remember nothing about the last eight days?"

She didn't answer.

"Are you trying to remember?"

"It's not as though I'm trying or not trying. There's nothing there but . . ."

His thick brow rose again. Katie didn't like it when he did that. He might as well shout *Liar!*

"Fear."

"Fear? You didn't act scared when I found you."

She didn't know what to say to that.

After a moment, he sighed as though he'd grown tired of her uncooperative behavior. Lifting the billing tab off the table, he gazed at Katie once more. "We'll talk again, Miss Thomas. If you remember anything at all, come see me in my office. It's at the top of the hill." He stood and strolled toward the counter to pay for her check.

Todd was wrong; Katie didn't like Sheriff Wade Murphy. He wasn't nice, neither was he generous. . . . All right, he paid for her breakfast, but he hadn't been nice about it.

The next morning, Katie worked in the kitchen smoothing icing on a chocolate cake. Todd came into the room, spied what she had baked, and made a straight line for the table.

Katie pointed the spatula at him. "You can't touch this cake."

"You didn't bake it for me?"

"No, I baked it for the sheriff."

Todd pushed his glasses farther up onto his nose. "Can't you give him a *piece* of cake?"

"Did you save my life?" She set the icing bowl on the table and placed a tin over the food.

"I had a hand in it. I nursed you back to consciousness."

Katie frowned at him. "What does that mean? You waited for me to wake up?"

"Yes."

"All right, I'll make you a pie for dinner. Will you open the door for me?"

Todd pushed the screen and stepped aside. When it took Katie nearly a minute to limp off the stoop, he asked, "Would you like me to deliver that for you?"

"I can manage," she answered with a pained expression.

Todd shrugged and returned to the kitchen.

Victor City was a pretty town, whitewashed and gleaming in the sunshine. It had been built on one wide and long road that led out of the mountains and ran along the South Platte River north of Sterling. Horses stood tethered outside each building. Buggies and buckboards sat in front of the grocer.

It did not take long to cross the road and stroll up the hill toward the split-rail fence enclosing the sheriff's yard. His office resembled a log house. Two rockers were placed on the front porch.

She knocked on the door and when the sheriff did not answer, Katie entered the neat office. The bare floors were swept clean. In the middle of the room sat a large desk with several chairs around it. Next to the desk and against the north wall hung a gun cabinet and hat rack.

Murphy's voice came from the backyard. Setting the

cake on his desk, Katie stepped through a door on the
other side of the office. Barney and Murphy had their
backs turned as they took target practice at tin cans scattered around the property. The sheriff turned just in time
to see Katie wince as she sat on the wooden step. He wore
blue jeans and a black shirt. "Hello," he called to her. At
least he sounded friendlier today.

"Miss Katie," Barney shouted, happy to see her.
"Watch this." His shot went wild and he missed the target. He managed to hit a pinecone off the nearest tree,
but Katie was sure that it wasn't what he aimed at, and
he pulled the funniest face when he did it that Katie
snickered—not at him, of course.

Barney stared red-faced at her.

"I'm sorry," she offered, but laughed again at how
silly he appeared with his sweet face conjuring up a
glare. To cover her bad manners, she smoothed her skirt.
"I laughed because I remembered something funny that
happened yesterday." Immediately she tried to think
of something that happened yesterday that they might
consider humorous. Hmm, she drew a blank.

The sheriff and Barney waited.

"Oh, I know. Todd rushed around the corner and tried
to open the hallway door. He didn't turn the knob in time
and slammed right into the wood."

Well, she had thought it was funny.

Murphy shook his head at Barney. "Don't worry
about it, boy. I've never known a woman yet who shoots
worth a nickel."

Barney turned triumphantly toward Katie. If the sheriff held such an opinion then so did he!

Katie struggled to her feet and stepped into the yard. "May I?" she asked Murphy, holding out her hand for his rifle.

"May you what?"

"The rifle, please."

Murphy and Barney looked at each other. Then they both started to laugh.

Katie took the weapon and after examining the single-shot .41, she pointed toward the tin can a hundred or so paces away. "Do you see that small patch of label below the lip of that can?" She jacked a shell into the chamber, put the rifle to her shoulder, and fired.

The can exploded.

Murphy and Barney collected the can that the bullet had mangled. When they stood beside her again, Katie told Barney, "Don't let the fact that I graduated from the Ellenboro's College for Ladies throw you. I have grit." When he continued to stare at her, she told him, "Close your mouth. You look like a trout."

"I have to show my dad," Barney declared and took off toward the gate.

Murphy kept pace beside her. "Children are easily impressed."

"Didn't I shoot worth a nickel, Sheriff?"

He stopped at the steps, reached beneath them to pull out a crate of tin cans, and tossed them around the yard. Some landed close, others landed far out into the field. "Now," he said, watching her with those gray-blue eyes, "impress me."

She studied the targets. "Eyes opened or shut?"

Murphy nodded. "Funny."

Katie lifted the weapon to her shoulder and hit every tin can in the yard—eyes open. She handed Murphy the rifle. "Ladies Champion of Westhill Rifle Association, four years running."

The sheriff didn't look as impressed as Katie thought he would. "Can you come inside for few minutes?"

Chapter Two

He held the door open for her and once Katie was halfway inside the office he asked, "Did you remember something to tell me, is that why you came here?"

She pointed to the tin-covered plate on his desk, "I brought you a cake." She watched him stare at it for a moment. The whole idea of befriending the sheriff suddenly seemed a terrible idea.

Murphy looked about as impressed with the cake as he had with her sharp shooting. "Thank you," he offered, and then tossed his hat onto a peg next to the gun rack. He pointed to a chair across from his desk. "Have a seat."

It was not an invitation and the uneasiness Katie had felt with him at the restaurant returned. She sat, but on the edge of the seat, and not comfortably.

His eyes slipped over her posture as he opened a drawer, took out a snub nose handgun, and placed it on the desk between them. "Do you recognize this weapon?"

"Should I?"

Murphy sat behind the desk, picked up the gun, and spun the cartridge. "You were carrying it when I found you."

"It's not mine."

He nodded and pulled open another drawer. "Todd removed these from Ben Raines' back." He tossed two mashed and mangled bullets onto the desk in front of her. "One of the men inside the coach, James Caldwell, was shot at close range with a snub nose and Charlie dug this"—he laid one more spent bullet on the desk—"out of the dead man I stumbled upon while I was searching for you. All the bullets came from the same gun." He tipped his chair onto two legs and laced his fingers behind his head. "The gun you carried."

Katie frowned at him. Did he think she shot those people?

"Is this your pistol?"

"I don't own a pistol."

"Yet you're a champion shot." His eyes held hers for a long moment while he rocked back and forth on the tipped legs of his chair.

"I'm a champion shot with a rifle. There's a difference."

"Do you own a rifle?"

"Of course."

"Where is it?"

The man never blinked, honestly.

"It's in Chicago."

"Are you sure you left it in Chicago?"

Katie heard the sarcasm in his voice. He did not believe that she could not remember the stage robbery. "I'm sure I left it in Chicago, Sheriff."

He righted the chair. "So really, that's the last thing you remember, isn't it?" Leaning his elbows on the desk, he picked up the gun once more. "It's difficult to believe you when you keep changing your story."

"What do you mean?"

"You said that the last thing you remembered was that you said good-bye to your aunt nine days ago. Now you say you're sure you left your rifle in Chicago."

"Well, it's not here. It has to be in Chicago."

He stood and pulled a rifle from the gun rack.

"That's my rifle!"

"I know," he said with a bright smile, but as quickly as his smile appeared it disappeared and he returned the rifle to the gun rack. "I found it in the dirt near the stagecoach. Todd told me it was yours and I asked if I could examine it."

"Had it been fired?"

"No."

"Then may I have it?"

"I don't think you should carry a weapon right now, Miss Thomas."

"Why not right now?"

He did not sit again but placed his hands on top of the desk and leaned toward her. "Right now I am investigating your story regarding the stage robbery."

"You believe I shot those men?"

It unnerved her the way he watched her.

"What possible reason would I have to shoot anyone?"

"I can think of ten thousand reasons why, such as the ten thousand dollars missing from the stage, which was carrying a money bag from Lincoln to Victor City."

"Money?"

His brow lifted. Could she say again how much she disliked it when he did that? "You didn't know there was money on the stage?"

"Why would I? I don't think stage drivers divulge that sort of thing." Exasperated, she got to her feet. "And for you information, I don't kill people for money, Sheriff."

"Why do you kill people?"

Sharp fear replaced her defensiveness. This man, this sheriff, thought she was a murderer. "I don't kill people at all," she whispered.

He moved around the desk to perch on its side. "Why did you leave college?"

The question brought her up short. "What?"

"I asked why you left . . . ?"

"I graduated."

"Wasn't there an incident that took place . . . ?"

"No."

In such close proximity, Katie saw every detail of Murphy's face. He had two freckles on his nose and a small scar beneath the grizzle on his chin. "You were nearly expelled, Miss Thomas, don't deny it. The headmistress and your aunt met with you . . ."

"What does any of that have to do with the stagecoach robbery?"

His shoulders squared up. "Stop interrupting me, Katie."

"Todd shouldn't have shared that with you." Her stomach twisted at the look on Murphy's face and she took a step backward. "It is none of your business."

He shoved off the desk. "His name is Anthony Ricci, isn't it?" He took a step toward her, keeping the distance between them uncomfortable. Katie felt cornered by him and no longer met his eyes. Instead, she averted her face and stared at his desk.

"You kept company with a felon, Miss Thomas, and that is my business because it sheds light on your character and your character is in question right now."

Murphy acted like so many other people in her life as of late. They all thought they knew everything before they asked the questions. With a lump in her throat, she whispered, "I never kept company with Anthony Ricci."

"Come off it." He stepped toward the desk and snatched a slip of paper from a box there. "I have a telegraph from Ellenboro's College for Ladies." He gazed at the paper. "A Mrs. Barnes answered my wire. Do you know Mrs. Barnes?"

"Yes."

"On the tenth of May you met with Headmistress Barnes and your aunt, Mrs. Volker." He read from the slip again. "Mrs. Volker grew upset to learn that you met with Mr. Ricci and admitted she introduced the two of you at her home. Mr. Ricci was engaged to your cousin, Nadine Volker, but your aunt said that she saw Anthony Ricci leave your bedroom after midnight during the week that he visited."

Katie's eyes stung and she felt one teardrop fall onto

her cheek. She rubbed at it hard with her fingers. Taking a step toward the door, she thought to run to Todd. He would listen to her.

Murphy took hold of her upper arm. "You may not have kept company with Mr. Ricci but you were up to something. Is your aunt lying?"

"No."

"Do you deny leaving the college residence after curfew and after the headmistress told you not to see Anthony Ricci again?"

"No."

He released her arm and stuffed the slip of paper into the top pocket of his shirt. "Now that we've verified that you had a relationship with a felon who's jailed for attempted murder, it follows that I should question you regarding the stage robbery. Since everyone else is dead or dying it is imperative, for the sake of your freedom, that you remember what happened." All of his anger appeared to have evaporated. He simply questioned her as if he were filling out the report. "Who were your accomplices?"

"I didn't have *accomplices.*"

"But someone helped you hold up the stagecoach. There are other bullets spent from different guns. You had accomplices. How many men?"

"I don't know how—"

"Was the dead man in the woods part of your gang?"

"I don't know a man—"

He picked up the snub nose pistol off the desk again. "Why did you try to shoot me after I told you my name?"

"I don't . . . What?"

He laughed softly but his eyes were cold and flat. "You and I are the only ones right now who know what happened in the woods that day, Katie. So why don't you tell me your version of the events."

Fear gnawed at her stomach. What had happened in the woods between the two of them? She had no idea what he was talking about and it was plain that he would not show any sympathy for her situation. Murphy was convinced that she was guilty and Katie did not know how to persuade him otherwise. "Am I under arrest?"

"No."

"Why not?"

"Your brother has a fine reputation in this town, Miss Thomas, and the last thing I want to do is arrest his sister for thievery and murder. My plan is to keep a close watch over you until the circuit judge comes to town in two weeks. I'll turn all the evidence over to him and he can set a trial in Denver. I'll take you there myself and it'll all be done quietly so that Todd doesn't suffer."

She supposed she should be grateful that. "So I can go home now?"

"You can go to Todd's house," he said, walking with her to the door. "But listen closely. Don't go near Ben Raines, not even if Todd asks you to sit with him. Make an excuse not to do it. You can't be alone with the man. Don't leave town, not one step, because if you do I will throw Todd's reputation to its fate and I'll arrest you right then."

Katie rushed to Todd's house and closed herself in her room. She fell onto the mattress and pulled a pillow to her chest. The sheriff thought she had robbed and murdered the men on that stage! How could he possibly think such a thing; did she *look* like someone who murdered people?

She got to her feet and paced the room. What was she going to do? Her first instinct was to run away. Katie reached for the trunk beneath her bed and pulled it out. Many of her clothes were still inside it. She would run away and in time the sheriff would figure out the mystery and—

Running away was for the guilty, and she was not guilty!

She moved toward the door. Todd would help her. He would talk to Murphy . . . except she didn't want to tell Todd. What would he think after all her trouble in Chicago? Perhaps he would believe the sheriff instead of her. She would be devastated if her own brother, her *beloved* brother, suspected her of murder.

Katie sat on the bed once more. Murphy said he wouldn't arrest her, and maybe she should simply leave things be until he had time to figure it out. Todd believed Wade Murphy was the finest lawman in the West. Did she have the nerve to trust him so much herself?

Worn out from the emotional turmoil, Katie reclined on the bed and fell asleep. She did not wake until the morning. A blanket covered her and she imagined Todd placed it over her sometime during the night. It was odd that she knew such peace in the morning. Perhaps all the tumult inside her had exhausted itself.

Todd did not act as though anything was wrong, so Katie concluded Murphy had not mentioned his suspicions to her brother. She certainly wouldn't mention them either. Todd would go stark raving if he thought she was in so much trouble. Ever since their parents died, Todd thought of himself as Katie's protector. What would he do now, steal her out of town so they would both be on the run?

He entered the kitchen behind Katie as she prepared vegetables for the stew that simmered on the hearth. He said, "I've invited Murphy to dinner tonight."

Katie turned toward him with the paring knife in hand. "What? Why?"

So much for acting as though everything was fine.

Todd stopped short and eyed the knife in her hand. Reaching out, he pushed the tip of it away from his chest with his index finger. "Not up to it? You told me you felt better this morning."

Katie chopped celery again.

"I think Murphy likes you," Todd said, standing at the counter and watching her. "He asks a lot of questions about you. The cake you made for him must've touched his heart."

"Trust me, Todd, there's nothing about me that touches Sheriff Murphy's heart." She chopped with vigor.

"You don't like Murphy?" When she did not answer, Todd exclaimed, "My lands, why not? He's a fine man, honest and brave. He's the sort of man you should watch for Katie Rebeccah, not some flash-in-the-sky character as you've hooked up with in the past."

He meant Anthony Ricci and Katie stopped axing the celery and stared at him. "Todd, we never talked about what happened in Chicago."

"And we don't have to. You said it was over and I believe you. Victoria and Nadine believe you as well, which is something, isn't it?" He leaned against the counter and smiled at her. "I received a letter from our dear auntie before you got here. She wrote that she was grateful that Nadine found out what sort of man Anthony was before she married him. She said that you helped to resolve it all nicely."

"What bothered me," he continued in a melancholy tone, "is that you didn't tell me what happened, Katie. I heard it all from Victoria."

"I was scared you'd get hurt, Todd. You would've stormed back to Chicago on the first stage."

"You don't think I was hurt anyway?" When she shook her head, he spoke over her. "I do understand, Katie. You went crazy over a man. It's understandable at your age."

"I didn't go crazy . . ."

"It was the chemicals in your body flaring inside of you. It was time to mate."

Her mouth fell open. "You did not just say *mate*. What am I, a champion horse, a pedigree pet dog?"

"No, of course not." He faced her. "It's just that I understand your interest. Now, take Sheriff Murphy. He is a good-looking man."

"Then you fix dinner for him."

"He's not really my type, but I'll tell you this." He leaned on the counter again and took a long stick of celery to chew. "If I were you I'd give Murphy a glance."

"You are not me."

He shook the vegetable at her. "I'm giving you straight talk, Kathryn."

She put the knife down and graced him with a cool look. "I'll cook, I'll act politely, and I'll retire early. I will not *glance* at Sheriff Murphy."

Katie had never known a more miserable circumstance than sitting in the sheriff's company while Todd spun yarns of her childhood misadventures. There was no doubt Todd's stories convinced Murphy that he had been correct to suspect her of an outlaw nature. Truly, she had been a spirited girl, but Todd made her out to be exceptionally so.

For example, she had never meant to steal Ned Taylor's horse. Well, she had meant to, but not criminally. If Ned had taken Katie home when she had asked him to, then she would not have had to draw a pistol and take his slow and dopey horse away from him in the first place.

Katie would not defend herself in front of Murphy, however, as it would appear oversensitive on her part. Therefore, she ate in silence and smiled at Todd when he referred to the time their aunt sat Katie down and explained that *ladies* should not use darning needles as weapons, even though Joey McNamara had stolen a lady's half-dollar that she received on her birthday.

Katie kept her eyes cast downward and handed the bowl of stew to Murphy. Did he sense her desire to change the subject? He said, "Marvin found Darryl's body out by Gulch Pass today. He must've been hit by one of the first bullets in the stage holdup."

Katie frowned and stared at the potato on her plate. Perhaps Todd should continue with her childhood misadventures.

"He was shot in the back and the bullet went right into his heart," Murphy continued. "Whoever shot him was an expert marksman."

She glanced in his direction and was immediately sorry because Murphy returned her look with a most distrustful expression on his face.

"Now that's just a shame," Todd replied. With his fork paused in midair, he asked Katie, "Do you remember anything about Darryl? He would've been riding shotgun." He placed the fork on his plate. "Darryl was a tall fellow with sandy blond hair. Mighty brave and loyal and trustworthy was Darryl Jones, may God bless his soul."

"I didn't shoot Darryl Jones, Sheriff," Katie said, then turned toward Todd and watched him frown.

"Why would you need to tell Murphy that? Of course you didn't shoot Darryl." Todd looked at their dinner guest. "Do you think she shot Darryl?"

Murphy finished chewing the meat in his mouth. He took his time to wipe his chin with the napkin and said, "I've never once thought you shot Darryl Jones."

Katie was relieved to hear it since she had lost track of whom the sheriff thought she had murdered.

Murphy sat back in his chair to fold the napkin and return it to his lap. "Darryl was shot from a long distance away. You were in the stagecoach."

Katie asked, "How do you know someone shot Darryl from far away?"

"Because his body was taken to the undertaker's

office and I had a look for myself. The bullet didn't come out the front of him. It's still in his heart." He leaned an elbow against the table. "Therefore, he was shot at from a long distance away."

"Now that makes sense," Todd replied, filling his mouth with bread. After he finished chewing, he said, "That makes two shooters then."

"Why two shooters?" Katie asked.

"Because the others were shot at close range."

"No," Murphy told him. "There were three shooters. The bullet that killed Darryl is different from the ones that shot Ben and Caldwell. Foster Garrett was killed with a third type of bullet."

Todd counted with him. "So there were two drivers, four people on the stage, three men holding up the stage . . ."

Again, Murphy corrected him. "No, two riders on horseback held up the stage, four people on the stage, and two men dead in the woods counting Bates."

"Bates?" asked Katie.

Murphy's eyes hardened. "My replacement, Sheriff Bates."

"Oh," she breathed out. "And the other man?"

Todd shook his head. "We don't know who he was. He might've been a hunter."

"Except that he dressed like a city man and didn't carry a weapon," Murphy explained.

"So he was on the stage?" she asked.

Murphy shrugged. "Or he was the point man."

"What is a point man?"

"You don't know what a point man is?"

Todd laughed. "She studied women's arts in college, Murphy. How would she know what a point man is?"

"I don't know. Katie seems like a clever girl to me."

Todd grinned at her. "I always thought so."

Murphy explained, "A point man is the man—or woman—who plans the holdup and he's the boss. He doesn't get his hands bloody. He waits for his men to do the job and then he collects his money."

"Why would anyone give him money if he doesn't do any of the work?"

"Because he's a manipulator. He's usually attractive and dominates everyone around him by using fear tactics, especially on woman."

"Murphy is an astute observer of behavior," Todd told Katie. "I've never yet seen him call it wrong. He has the best gut instincts around."

Katie got to her feet. "Oh, I'm sure you'll be found wrong one day, Sheriff." She lifted her plate. "I'll get dessert."

Murphy stood too. "I'll help you."

Todd acted so pleased that Katie did not object. When she walked into the kitchen, she let the swinging door fly back at Murphy. He caught it with his forearm and followed her into the room. She asked, "Aren't you worried that I am going to pull a darning needle on you?"

"I can defend myself. Knife?"

"Please."

Murphy offered her the long-handled blade and leaned on the table to watch her cut into the blueberry pie. "So you were a live coal growing up?"

"Live coal?" She cut the pie into eight slices. "I wasn't

a live coal." She lifted one slice onto a small plate and handed it to him. "Todd stretched those stories."

"I've never known Todd to stretch stories." He put a clean fork on the plate. "I find it interesting that you didn't tell him about our conversation yesterday in my office."

"What's so interesting about that?"

"That you didn't tell him."

She scooped another piece of pie. "If Todd thought I was in real trouble, he would fret."

"I've never known Todd to fret."

"Perhaps you don't know as much as you think you do."

He smiled and did not reply. His eyes remained alert though, as if her every word and her every move meant something to him.

"I know you followed me today into the grocer's. I saw you studying a cinnamon canister as though it contained a cure for smallpox."

"I look at my food before I buy it."

"You watched me."

He shrugged. "You're a beautiful girl."

"Mm-hmm, then you followed me into the telegraph office."

"I had to speak to Earl."

She set the knife aside and rewrapped the pie top. "Mm-hmm, and what pulled you into the dressmaker's shop?"

"Mary is a better tailor than Tim Marlow and I asked her to sew a couple of shirts for me." He took two of the plates and moved toward the swinging door.

"And you just needed to pick them up while I was there to be fitted?"

"I just needed to pick them up."

She followed him into the dining room again. Todd stood at the front door. "It's a fine evening. Let's sit on the porch with our dessert."

Katie set her plate on the table. "You two go ahead. I'll clear the table and set the kitchen aright."

She was not surprised when Murphy handed his plate to Todd and turned toward her to say, "I'll help you."

Todd grinned.

"No, thank you. You're our *guest*," she said forcefully, trying to stress the point. "Please join Todd."

Todd shook his head. "I need to check on Ben, and Murphy loves to stay busy. Let him help you, Katie."

Once Todd moved toward the stairs, Katie glared at Murphy. With a bowl of potatoes in one hand, she said, "I don't need your help."

He lifted the roast plate. "You're playing standoffish to make me more interested, aren't you?"

Her mouth fell open at the suggestion.

Todd's footsteps continued up the stairs.

"Yes, yes I am." She grabbed the breadbasket and stepped into the kitchen. Murphy brought in the rest of the tableware while she stored the food in the cold box. She held a serving spoon and shook it at him. "You're harassing me. Isn't there a law against that sort of thing?"

"No."

"Well there should be." She placed the utensils in a pan and poured water over them. "These need to soak so I'll say good night, Sheriff."

"It's too early to sleep. Come for a walk with me instead."

"No, thank you. It was a pleasure to have you for dinner." Footsteps pounded overhead and Katie frowned at the ceiling. "I'm sure my brother will keep you company on the porch."

She heard Todd's footsteps on the stairs again. He suddenly burst into the kitchen with her cream-colored shawl in one hand. "It's cool tonight if you're going walking."

"We're not going walking!"

Grinning, Murphy took the shawl from Todd and draped it around Katie's shoulders. "We won't stay out long." He offered his arm. "I promise."

"Take your time," Todd told him. "I'll finish cleaning."

The evening air smelled pleasant. Crickets buzzed. Lanterns lit the wide gravel thoroughfare and across the street dishes clanged and glasses tinkled as low voices sounded inside Marigold's Kitchen. Katie had taken Murphy's arm to be mannerly but the nearness of him made her heart pound hard in her chest—and not in any way romantically. Murphy had such a powerful presence that it unsettled her. He had placed his hand on top of hers as if he thought she might try to run away from him.

First they strolled northward, but before they reached the saloon, Murphy led her across the road and then walked toward the south again. Lamps lit the interior buildings. Chicago used electric light but Victor City had no such luxury. Lanterns dangled from walkway poles and from low branches in the tallest trees.

"Why did you want me to walk with you?"

He glanced down at her. Half his face was shadowed, half was touched by the lantern light. She realized again how attractive the man was. Clean-shaven this evening, his jaw appeared cut and chiseled and she noticed he had a cleft in his chin. He said, "No reason."

"Then I would like to go home."

"Let's go farther. You're an able and healthy girl." His hand tightened over hers. "Besides, it isn't often I have such a beautiful woman on my arm."

Katie turned to walk with him again. "Fine, but I want you to stop saying that I'm beautiful and lovely and how I act standoffish to interest you."

His gray eyes slipped over her features and he dropped his voice. "But I am interested in you, Katie. Everything about you fascinates me."

"I know why you're interested in me, so stop pretending that it's something other than an investigation. I want to go home."

He shook his head and pulled her along the walk. "I want to show you something." He propelled her up the hill toward the coroner's office. "I want you to take a look at Darryl."

Katie came to a fast halt. "Darryl's dead."

"Mm-hmm."

"What's there to see?"

He rounded on her. "You said that you don't remember what happened in the woods and I thought this might prove to be constructive. If you recognize Darryl then you might remember other details."

"Yes, I see. You're very clever."

"I like to think so." He pulled her, stiff-legged, along the walk again and then toward an alley. "I should've had you take a look at the man from the woods before Charlie pushed dirt on him. I guess we could exhume the body."

"Oh, no need for that," Katie told him in a weak voice.

"You don't strike me as the type of girl to swoon over the remains of the dead."

It would require a great deal of imagination to take his statement as a compliment.

The dark yard bumped up against a wooded area. Funerary boxes lined the outside of the building. After taking the steps to the porch, Murphy opened the door. Katie followed him into the dark room and waited while he struck a match on the sole of his boot to light the wick of a wall sconce.

The candle illuminated a sterile room with bare floors. A cabinet stood against one wall and a tall-legged table sat in the center of the room. There, a hallow-cheeked cadaver lay, still in death's pose, with legs crooked and arms bent and stiff. Murphy lit another lamp and faced Katie. "Do you recognize him?"

"No."

"Take a good look. You are gazing everywhere but at his face."

Taking a breath for courage, Katie glanced at Darryl Jones. She did recognize him. It was only a flash but she recalled how he helped her out of the coach by offering his hand. He had been smitten with her and grown obvious about it.

"Well?"

Katie shrugged. "He drove the coach."

"No flashes of memory? No hints of what happened out there?" He sounded as though he mocked her, but when Katie looked at him, Murphy showed no emotion at all.

She said, "We had stopped at a depot. He helped me out of the coach and then told me that I had a small time to eat and freshen myself. He didn't want me to go too far. He acted concerned . . ."

"Which depot?"

"I don't know."

"Did you talk to anyone?"

Katie nodded at Darryl. "Only him."

"You talked to Darryl?"

"Yes, and I ate a biscuit."

Murphy rubbed his face hard. "It amazes me that you can remember that you ate a biscuit but you can't tell me what occurred later in the day. What happened when the men stopped the coach? Did Foster die right away?"

"I don't know Foster."

"Foster was a nineteen-year-old boy coming home from college. I imagine that he found you attractive. He was smitten with every girl he met. I had to tell his family that he died. His mother may never recover. She went completely hysterical."

"Oh . . ." The thought of the woman's agony stirred her compassion.

"And why was Ben Raines shot in the back? Did he run with the money?" Exasperated when she did not answer, Murphy said, "Can you tell me anything, Katie, that I don't already know?"

"There's someone gazing in the window watching us."

Murphy spun around toward the only window in the room. His hand went to the gun on his hip. "What?"

"I saw someone at the window."

He stepped across the room and pulled the door open. Katie followed him.

"Stay here," he instructed as he went down the steps and then slid along the building.

Keeping her back to the same wall and with both hands on her wrap, Katie glided along after him. She did a good job of staying light on her toes right up to the moment Murphy stopped short and she tiptoed into the back of him. "I told you to stay inside."

"With the dead body?"

Through the dim light, she saw the outline of Murphy's jaw and the way it squared. "Who looked into the window?"

"How should I know?"

"Did you lie to me?"

"Why would I lie to you?"

"To leave the room."

Katie shook her head. "I saw someone's face in the window, Murphy."

"Then why didn't you scream?"

She wrinkled her nose at him. "I was standing next to the sheriff. Why would I scream?" She pulled at her wrap. "Oh, wait. That would be a good reason to scream, wouldn't it?"

He threw her an irritated look and then studied the dirt beneath the window. Katie was no lawman but she saw boot prints there in the low light. Murphy's eyes followed the tracks toward the woods. Then he gazed at Katie. "Go home."

"By myself?"

"It's just across the road."

"Some date you are," she told him, ready to move away.

Murphy took her elbow and pulled her backward. "Did you want a kiss good night?" His voice sounded husky and then he laughed at her shocked expression. "I'm willing."

Katie jerked away from him.

Murphy laughed again and then studied the ground and the prints. He moved toward the trees.

For a long moment, Katie stared after him. Then she spun around and raced toward Todd's house. After she slammed the door behind her, she faced Todd and pointed out the window. "There's something seriously wrong with that man."

"Why, what happened?" He glanced up from a medical tome he had been browsing.

"He wanted to kiss me!"

Todd grinned. "What's wrong with that?"

Katie remembered then that Todd did not know Murphy thought she murdered half the men in the county. "Never mind." She climbed the stairs to the sound of his laughter.

Chapter Three

 S he went into the kitchen as the hall clock chimed six in the morning. Todd still slept. The air felt cool through Katie's long-sleeved blouse and she took a half apron from the cabinet and fit it over her waist. The puncheon floor creaked when she ambled toward the cold box. Today she and Todd would breakfast on bread, potatoes, hung beef, and strong tea. Katie planned to make enough to save for lunch and dinner. Todd's kitchen had a wood-burning oven and she stoked it to heat it to bake more bread.

The one thing Katie missed about her aunt's home in Chicago was the phonograph. She sang "Amazing Grace," as she worked and then "The Sweet Bye and Bye." She did not sing well, but no one was awake to listen to her, or so she thought.

Moving toward the root cellar, she descended the steps to retrieve the potatoes while singing "Nobody

Knows the Trouble I've Seen." She took the steps again only to stop when she saw Sheriff Murphy in the doorway. He said, "Good morning, Katie."

It was a sin to Moses the way the man kept springing up! "Goodness," she said, clutching her heart with her free hand.

"You're surprised to see me?"

Katie climbed the remaining steps.

Murphy did not move away from the doorjamb but continued to watch her in the low light shining through the kitchen windows. His face looked shadowy . . . like the character he was!

She told him, "I'd worry if you didn't show up, Sheriff. Somebody might've shot you in the night, or knifed you, or strangled you with my purse strap."

He moved out of her way, grinning largely at her.

She moved to the table and placed potatoes on the chopping board. Grabbing a pot from overhead, she meant to walk out to the well and draw water for boiling. But suddenly she remembered something. "Did you find anyone in the woods last night?"

"Cold tracks," he answered, leaning at the counter. "Is Todd awake?"

"No." She headed for the screen door ready to show the sheriff out. "I'll tell him that you called for him."

"I'll wait."

"Good," she told him and stepped out of the house. She would spend all morning pumping water if she needed to and Murphy could stand in the kitchen if he liked.

Except that he followed her out the screen door.

Katie winced when she saw him. Murphy laughed

and leaned against the step railing to watch her. "Katie, you give me the impression that you don't like me."

She didn't answer and worked the pump handle furiously. With her pot full of water, she moved toward him again. He wore a brown shirt that was only a shade lighter than his dark hair that fell in waves on either side of his face. In the morning light she saw how thick his lashes were that framed his gray-blue eyes. He said, "Do you know that I could not wait for you to come to Victor City so that I could meet you?"

She did not tell him that she had wanted to meet him too. Todd had not done Murphy's appearance justice, for he spoke more about how the sheriff was a man of integrity, high principles, and of unvarnished honesty. Ha!

Murphy continued, "Todd told me all about you and by his descriptions I thought you must have fallen straight out of heaven."

They stood only a foot apart and Katie watched him closely. Did he want to be friends now? Was he flirting? He appeared relaxed there with his arm on the rail and his boots crossed at the ankles. "I saw the picture you sent to Todd, was it two months ago?" He grabbed his heart as though it picked up pace. "And I knew that he lied when he said that you were as ugly as a frog."

"What are you doing, Sheriff?"

"I'm only passing time until Todd comes downstairs." He pushed off the railing and took the pot from her hands. "And finding out how quickly you can be manipulated by compliments."

"By a point man?"

"I knew you were a clever girl."

Angry now, she snapped, "You didn't fool me, Murphy. I didn't fall for any of that."

"Sure. That's why you've gone pink in the cheeks." He stepped into the kitchen ahead of her and set the pot on the hearth. "What's next?" he asked as though he intended to help her with breakfast.

"What's next is that you find someone else to irritate." She peeled the largest potato and grinned at him.

He raised one brow.

She stopped grinning.

"You're somewhat melodramatic, Miss Thomas."

How did she act melodramatic? She did not ask him why he said it because his next question proved he was leading up to something.

"Todd told me of your interest in the theater."

"I enjoy it."

"You love to playact, don't you? You were in a production in Chicago, isn't that right?"

"Acting, not *playacting* and it was *Twice Told Tales*," she informed him.

He chuckled softly. "*Twice Told Tales*? That sounds about right."

She stopped peeling the vegetable. "What are you getting at?"

Shrugging innocently, he offered, "It's sometimes hard to determine when an actress is performing or when she's speaking for herself."

Narrowing her eyes on him, she asked, "You think that I acted when I told you that I didn't remember the stage holdup?" She peeled the potato again. "You're incredible, Sheriff."

He shrugged again, feigning humility.

She did not praise him. "You're a gossipmonger."

"I am a what?"

"Gossipmonger. Everything Todd told you about me you repeat and use as evidence against me."

He pushed off the counter and stepped toward the table. "Then set me straight."

She lifted a shoulder. "Whatever I say you twist around to make it fit your version of what happened out there. For some reason you want to find me guilty."

He stood just across the table. "Why would I do that?"

"I *know* why." She took up the last potato to peel. "You're resentful because you didn't get to purchase the colts you wanted and you're resentful because your replacement for sheriff was killed. You're stuck here in Victor City dealing with drunks, pickpockets, and rowdies instead of out in the open country raising stallions." She smiled at his rigid features. "Todd tells me things too, Murphy, and what I think is that your gut instincts are colored by your cynicism and malice."

"I'm not cynical . . ."

"But you are, Murphy. You're tainted and you're not looking at things clearly."

"Well this is rich coming from you, who claims not to remember—"

"Oh," she interrupted, wagging the peeler at him, "that's another thing: I pointed a gun at you and you're angry." She raked the potato, delighted to make her point, but then softened her tone. She supposed she would be angry if someone pointed a gun at her. She said, "I do see your view, Sheriff. If someone pointed a gun in my face and then once the lightning struck they dove for it . . . I'd be mad too."

She collected the peeled spuds and rounded the table to drop them into the pot of water. She studied Murphy after she fit the lid on top. He had gone so silent.

"You made a mistake."

"I did?"

He nodded. "You did."

She tried to remember what she had said. "You told me I pointed the gun at you!"

Murphy shook his head. "Acting—it is a good thing you gave it up." He refitted the Stetson and walked toward the screen door. "I'll see Todd later."

The absolute arrogance of the man stunned her. The way he had said *You made a mistake.* What did he mean? She walked to the screen door and watched Murphy step out of the yard.

Katie napped in the afternoon trying to get rid of her headache. She was not sure how long she slept or what it was that woke her. Had someone spoken? Katie rolled off the bed and gazed out the window. She saw the sheriff's office to her right and Murphy standing on the porch. Thinking it was safe to return downstairs, she stepped into the hallway.

A groan sounded behind her. It came from Ben Raines' room. The door stood partially open. Was Todd inside? She peeked into the room.

Drawn shades kept the spare bedroom dark. Katie saw Ben Raines through the dim light. His breathing was heavy, erratic. He moaned again. Was he awake? Katie bit her lip. Should she talk to him? Would he tell her what happened during the stage robbery?

She crept silently into the room and shut the door. Her heart nearly beat out of her chest when a board creaked beneath her boots. Moving closer to the bed, Katie saw that Ben Raines was broad through the chest and probably in his late twenties. She studied his face. He had thick lashes and light brown hair . . . and did not look familiar at all.

Ben's head moved on the pillow and Katie touched his shoulder. "Ben?" Leaning over him, she repeated, "Ben, it's me, Katie." He might not know her from anybody but she thought she would at least introduce herself.

It looked as though he tried to speak. And then, in a most incredible volume, he shouted, "THE GIRL!"

Katie fell backward off the bed. She caught herself on the bedspread and pulled to her feet.

"THE GIRL," he cried again. "THE GIIIIRRLLL."

She hurried around the bed and rushed toward the door. Murphy could not catch her in this room!

Footsteps on the stairway caused her to turn around again, race toward the bed, and duck behind it.

The door crashed open.

She lay flat and scooted beneath the bed.

Murphy said, "He's waking."

Now how in the blue-eyed world did he get here so quickly?

Todd moved toward the bed. "Ben? Ben, old buddy?"

Katie winced when someone sat on the bed and the mattress moved toward her face. She need not worry about going to jail any longer. She would smother to death beneath this corn-silk mattress.

"YOU HAVE TO FIND HER!"

Murphy asked, "What about the girl, Ben? What about Katie Thomas?"

Now wasn't that just like the sheriff to think Ben hollered about her? Did the man have no bottom to his suspicious nature? If she had a knife, she would stab him in the boot.

Ben's voice grew more agitated. "She has the money."

"Easy," said Todd.

Ben quieted then. *Oh sure,* Katie thought, *go back to sleep after you have besmirched my good name!*

Murphy asked, "Is Katie still in her room?"

"She hasn't come out all afternoon. Why?"

The sheriff did not answer and Katie saw two pairs of boots step out of the room. She waited. Then Murphy called her name, presumably at her bedroom door, and when she did not answer, they moved downstairs.

Katie scrambled out from beneath the bed when she heard Todd call her name. She got to her feet to tiptoe around the bed. On the second floor, the veranda wrapped all the way around the house. If she could get outside and climb down one of the posts, Murphy might not find out that she'd been in Ben's room.

The window stuck halfway opened and Katie had to squeeze her way out of it. Straightening her skirt, she peered over the railing. People milled about on the street but no one paid attention to her.

She thought to return to her room but saw Todd's shadow pass behind the window. Murphy would be next.

Finding the nearest post, Katie hiked her leg over the railing. The toe of her boot hit the pole and she grabbed the beam with both hands, then wrapped her feet at the bottom beneath the eaves. She worked downward and when she nearly touched bottom, she heard Murphy's voice above her head.

"Katie?" He shoved the window all the way up and stepped onto the veranda.

She let go of the post and landed hard on the ground.

"Stay exactly where you are," he warned. His hand rested on the grip of his gun.

Todd climbed through the window next and stared at her in disbelief. "Kathryn Rebeccah Thomas."

Thickets and trees lay to her left and she clambered toward them.

"Stop," Murphy warned.

He wouldn't shoot her, would he?

A bullet ricocheted off the tree beside her. Another shot rang out and Katie hit the ground of the woods. She started to crawl. When she got past the sage bush, she stood and started to run.

She had done this before, she realized. It rained the last time and thunder exploded in the air.

Katie slowed and glanced around her. A clear blue sky held no hint of rain. Not a breeze stirred the leaves. Why had she heard thunder? Her heart raced faster knowing that a significant memory lay just within her grasp. She started to run again and found a trail.

Barney stood by the fence and when he saw Katie, he called out to her and waved.

She skidded to a stop and tried to compose herself.

She did not want to scare him. "Hiya, Barney. What goes on here?"

"I'm digging for worms. The fish are biting in the calm part of the creek."

"Do you know what I'd like to do?"

"You can go fishing with me, if that's what you're asking."

Katie caught her breath. "No, I don't want to fish. I'd like to see the spot where the stagecoach stopped. I think I might remember something if I see the setting. Will you help me?"

Barney grinned. "Yes, ma'am." He dropped the worm can for the more rousing idea. "We can ride double on my horse."

Katie's eyes followed his pointing finger. There by the oak tree stood a gray mare. *Thank you, Lord,* Katie prayed. *Always deeper in your debt.*

"I think . . . there!" Barney shouted, excited to find the wheel tracks still visible. He slipped off his horse, Matilda, and ran to examine the ruts.

It was all Katie could do to get off the horse. Her ribs ached again and her bottom hurt now. "I'm right behind you," she called to Barney.

"You jumped from the coach on this side," Barney announced, playacting his version of the scene. "Bullets whizzed all around you and you hid behind this tree." He chose a slender elm and dove behind it. "Then you shot it out with the bandits." He came from behind cover and pointed his finger to pull the trigger of his hand.

"Nonsense," she said, picking her way across the uneven ground. "I would never hide behind a tree. I came out with pistols blazing in a spectacular battle."

Barney did not look impressed. "I thought you didn't remember what happened."

"I don't exactly. I just know how I would handle the situation." She smiled at the boy and then turned to study the wheel tracks. Yep, they were wheel tracks all right. Katie looked around but didn't see anything that unlocked her memory. She stared left and then right. "East," she instructed Barney.

"Victor City is north of here."

"Doesn't the Overland Trail run east of here?"

"Yes, ma'am. How did you know that?"

"I don't know exactly."

The tall ponderosa pine trees blocked the azure sky. In full daylight, the wood appeared overcast and dim. Katie and Barney crunched their way through the dead leaves on the forest floor and their legs brushed the undergrowth. Katie wished she'd had the foresight to wear pants instead of a long skirt and button-up blouse. But, she'd had no idea that she would be a fugitive that afternoon. Ellenboro's College for Ladies had not prepared her for such an event.

They walked for a time when Katie said, "Nothing— I don't remember any of this."

"Maybe we should start to run around all crazy-like," Barney suggested. "That's how the sheriff said he found you."

Hands on hips, she faced the boy. "Did he, now?"

Barney did not notice her indignation. He bounded

off, running in a circle, and waving his hands in the air. Katie frowned at him. He looked ridiculous. Yet the oddest thing happened when she heard the quick thrashing sound of Barney's boots. Pinpricks of nerves crossed her neck and shoulders. Dread filled her chest until she thought her heart would burst.

Barney stopped running and turned to look at Katie. "Did you hear something, Miss Katie?"

Pulling herself together for Barney's sake, she told him, "I'm just thinking . . ."

"Did you hear that?"

Katie glanced at the boy. "Just you bouncing up and down like a hayseed." The troubled look on Barney's face made her pause though, and she tilted her head to listen. The woods had grown silent. Even the crickets quieted.

Barney returned to her side and took her hand. Together they watched the woodland. Katie sneaked a peek at the boy. His brown eyes were wide and his body had grown taut as a bowstring.

This was not good. She had been counting on Barney to be the brave one on this excursion. Squaring herself, she knew that the worst thing they could do was to let their imaginations get the better of them. They needed to stay calm. "Bear?" she asked, feigning idle curiosity.

"Maybe, but I think it's smaller."

Katie relaxed. "Snake?"

"Bigger than a snake."

"Cougar?"

Barney's hand tightened and they gazed at each other. "I'd like to go back to town now," he said and Katie nodded. She did not want to go back to Victor City empty-handed but she did not want to stay in the woods either.

A twig snapped to their left.

Their exodus sounded loud: crunching leaves, breaking brushwood, heavy breathing . . . and that was only Katie. Barney had his own style of retreat: hollering like a tomfool.

Chancing a look behind them, Katie did not see a cougar or a bear or even a snake, but their momentum would not abate until she collided with a tall and thin man who stepped out of the trees.

Katie sprawled sideways into the leaves.

The man grabbed Barney by the shoulders and pulled him backward. With his free hand, he pulled a knife from his belt. "I have been waiting for you, Katie." Dressed in patched and grubby clothing, he looked sweaty and drunk and he smelled like a hot donkey. "It's time to go find the money." He waved a long knife at her. His tone sharpened. "I said come on, Katie."

Barney's eyes widened when the knife flashed near his face.

"I don't know what you're talking about, mister," she told him, getting to her feet.

"You don't know what I'm talking about?" He snatched a handful of Barney's hair and placed the knife at the boy's throat. "You better start knowing or your little friend here is going to get hurt."

"Let him go and I'll show you where I put the money." She could do no such thing, of course, but she thought to get Barney out of harm's way.

The man seemed to think it over. A single bead of sweat ran past his left ear and curved into his spiny beard. A moment later, he shoved Barney to the ground. He pointed the knife at Katie and stepped toward her.

"Go on," she told Barney. "Get on your horse and get back to town."

A pistol blast rent the air.

The man jumped backward as the knife flew out of his hand. He stared in the direction of the blast as he pulled a small gun from the back of his belt.

Katie turned to see Sheriff Wade Murphy standing a hundred yards away with his feet planted firmly, his pistol sighted, and his aim set on their attacker. Relief flooded her tight muscles. For the first time, Katie was happy to see the sheriff.

Suddenly an arm went around her neck. The man's forearm squeezed her throat as cold metal pressed into her temple. He shouted, "Well, looka here. Everyone wants to join the fun!" He laughed hard and then spat on the ground. "I'll shoot her, Sheriff, I swear I will."

"I would think that through if I were you," Murphy warned. He had not moved and his face was full of fury. "If you kill her I'll have an easier shot."

The man laughed again. His whole body shook, causing his arm to squeeze tighter on her throat. "I guess you think you're some kind of hero, is that it? You've got all the guts in the world." He pushed the derringer roughly against Katie's face.

"Miss Katie," Barney whisper. She did not know that he had picked up a rock—apparently neither did her captor. The boy shrieked, "You let her go!" and threw the rock straight at the man's head.

Katie fell into the leaves again when the man grabbed his face and spun toward Barney. Another bullet exploded and tore through the man's shoulder. He fell to one knee and then scrambled toward a bush for cover. The man pulled the trigger, aiming at Murphy, but the sheriff was on the move and dropped to roll. Before Murphy got to his feet again, the man fled. He scurried through the forest like a rabbit chased by a hound.

Murphy followed him but moments later he stomped into the clearing and reached for Katie. "Barney," he said without looking at the boy. "Matilda is waiting for you over there next to Indigo. Start moving that way." When Barney shuffled ahead of them, Murphy pulled Katie closer. "Tell me who that fellow is."

"I don't know."

She tried to take a step backward but Murphy yanked her closer. "I heard him say your name. He knows you. Why would a thug like him know you?"

"I don't . . ."

Murphy dragged her by the arm through the brush and toward his horse. "You're under arrest, Miss Thomas."

She started to struggle then. "I came out here to remember what happened to me."

"Tell it to the judge." He lifted her roughly into the saddle. "You're under arrest because you went into Ben Raines' room after I told you to stay away from him. You left town after I told you not to." He kneed the horse forward. "You're under arrest because you're a suspect in the death of Nathan Bates, Foster Garrett, James Caldwell, and Theodore Moon. You're the suspected accomplice in Darryl Jones' death; you're suspected to have mortally wounded Ben Raines. You're under arrest for stealing thousands of dollars from the OM Stage Line and the Victor City Bank . . ."

"You told that man you know where the money is, Miss Katie," Barney insisted, riding slowly on the horse next to them. "Why don't you just tell the sheriff?"

Murphy pulled hard on the reins to stare at Barney. "WHAT?" Then he jerked Katie closer and bent to see her face. "What?"

Barney sounded scared. "Miss Katie tried to help me, Sheriff. She didn't do anything wrong."

Murphy ignored him. "Where's the money?"

She gave up the struggle. "I don't know."

"You brought the boy out here and endangered his life. Did you plan to kidnap him and hold him for ransom until you got away?"

Katie did not answer.

"Tell me where you hid the money and things will go easier for you." When she did not answer again, he growled "Come on" to Barney and kicked the horse into a gallop.

"Murphy, you can't put Katie in jail," Todd objected. He had been waiting in the sheriff's office for their return. Now he followed Murphy and Katie as Murphy yanked open the cell door. "Will you please tell me what's going on?"

"I will," the sheriff answered as he propelled Katie

into the jail cell and locked the door. "Come with me," he told Todd.

Katie grabbed the bars. "Todd. I didn't do anything. Don't believe him. I didn't do it."

Todd appeared torn. He acted as though he wanted to stay with her but needed to go with the sheriff. "Let me sort this out, Katie." He started for the next room but spun around. His blond hair fell across his brow and his blue eyes glared furiously. "I don't know what sort of trouble you're in, Kathryn, and I don't know why you tore off into the woods like you did, but I'll tell you what—"

"Come on," Murphy interrupted, grabbing him by the shoulder. "Sit at my desk."

He left the outer door open and Katie heard them move about in the other room. A wooden chair squeaked when one of them sat. Then a new voice spoke. Katie guessed Barney's mother had entered the room because the woman sounded hysterical. "Why did you let that woman run around this town if you suspected she had something to do with that stage holdup?"

Chair legs slid backward and Todd shouted her down. "What are you talking about?"

Another voice spoke, Mr. Crowe's by the gist of his words: "My boy just got through telling me about a man in the woods who held a knife to his throat."

It grew too loud to distinguish voices after that and Katie sat on the bench in the corner and covered her face with her hands.

Chapter Four

Victor City had been built in a valley near the South Platte River. Settlers only removed enough trees to squeeze fourteen buildings on each side of a wide road, which cut out of the wilderness to run north and south. Originally constructed around a stage outpost, it grew to its current size of about three hundred people, including those who lived on outlying ranch lands. Katie saw a perfect view of the west side of town. It was perfect in the sense that the jailhouse stood on a slight hill that afforded a good view. It was not so perfect in the sense that Katie had to stand tiptoe on her cot to see out the long and barred window.

She enjoyed watching the townspeople go about their business. Men stood outside of the leathery smoking and chewing tobacco. Next door sat the grocers. It was two stories and painted yellow with baskets of vegetables lining the porch. Sunflowers grew along the side of

58

the building. Katie loved sunflowers because they made her think of open fields and freedom.

The drugstore and shoe shop stood next to the grocer's, then the gunsmith's, and beside it was Dr. Todd Thomas' Surgery and Apothecary. A dark and curly-haired fellow rang the bell on the front porch and waited for Todd to answer. Beside the surgery was the dressmaker's shop. It was Katie's favorite building. The brick shop had a tall front door painted such a shiny red color that it still looked wet. Bolts of brightly colored fabric filled the windows and a white picket fence enclosed the yard full of daisies, bluets, and cosmos.

The seamstress was two or three years older than Katie and there was no way to describe her other than cute as a button. Mary Billingsworth stood just over five feet and had a voluptuous build. A pale brown mass of curls framed her round face and a slight lisp disrupted her speech. What interested Katie most about Mary was that Mary seemed crazy over Todd. When Todd crossed the street to visit Katie, the woman's face peaked out from behind her lacy curtains. At least two or three times a week Mary took Todd a casserole or something sweet she'd baked.

Todd was oblivious to it, as usual. Katie remembered how the girls at school had liked Todd. Although he was attractive with his pale hair and blue eyes, she was sure it was his glasses that attracted the opposite sex; they made him look educated and deliberate.

Two days ago, Katie had asked Todd, "What about Mary?"

"What about her?" he had replied grumpily.

"I don't know, she's such a pretty girl and many of the men here get their clothing from her shop instead of the tailor's place at Blue Bells."

"What men?"

Katie kept her reply purposely vague. "I don't know all their names. But you're right. They may not be interested in her because she's young and beautiful. I hear she's an excellent seamstress. Even the sheriff buys his shirts from her."

He frowned then, agitated. "Murphy does?"

After Todd departed, Katie hopped onto the cot and watched him walk across the road. He stopped halfway and then stepped toward Mary's place. Katie smiled in delight.

Adjacent to the dressmaker's shop stood Blue Bells Tenement. Neighboring Blue Bells' place was Big Buck's Saloon and across the street were more businesses that Katie could not see, but she knew there was a sawmill, a post and telegraph office, Victor City Bank, and Marigold's Kitchen. Right next to the jailhouse was the undertaker's office. Charlie probably had not been a hardworking man until the last week and a half. He seemed to appreciate the business and tipped his hat at Murphy often. Ghoulish, Katie thought. She had nick-named him Charlie Ghoul.

A splendid church stood behind the sheriff's office. It rose on the hilltop and stood tallest of all the town buildings. Its steeple pointed heavenward as a testimony to the proper perspective in life. Katie wished to visit the church someday. She just hoped it wasn't for her own funeral.

She sat on the cot and waited for her dinner. It had turned hot again and the evening was as still as a pan of water on a level porch. Crickets droned and the sun went down.

Murphy finished stirring the pot of beans on the small stove in the corner of his office and scooped a ladleful onto two plates, then added a chunk of cornbread to each. He had only jailed a woman one other time in his stint as sheriff. He didn't like it any better now than then. Katie needed special arrangements. Take a man, any man, and he would sit and rot in his clothing and Murphy would never hear a complaint, but Katie Thomas, she had to have privacy and her hairbrush and the combs to put her hair back into . . . He tapped the jail room door open with his boot and walked into the room.

Katie didn't turn when he first entered. She appeared small and forlorn resting on the cot. Her pale hair took on a golden glow and it made a circle of light around her lovely face. That was what a woman prisoner did to him! Feelings of compassion rose up inside of Murphy, along with a charitable feeling of protectiveness.

Until she spoke.

"What a curious combination of odors," she said, putting her feet on the floor.

"It's pork and beans."

Pushing off the cot, Katie walked toward the bars. "I hope it's better than the chicken you fried last night. My piece looked like a burned stick out of the fire. Tasted like it too . . ."

He narrowed his eyes on her.

"Delicious as it was," she added demurely and took the plate of food from beneath the bars and walked toward the cot. "Do you think it'd be all right if I took a bath this evening?"

"You can wash in the morning."

"I'd sleep better if I had a hot bath."

He took a breath to keep his temper in check. "This isn't a hotel."

Katie sat again and shoved the beans with her fork. Something had been needling her and she thought to bring up the subject in hopes of getting Murphy to think logically and decently about the entire stage robbery. "Why did the man in the woods pull a knife on me if he's my accomplice?"

"He didn't pull the knife on you. He pulled it on Barney," the sheriff answered, logically and decently. Turning from her, he studied the lantern on the wall.

"But why? If the man is my accomplice, why pull a weapon at all?"

He adjusted the wick. "Because you hid the money. The man wanted his share. He pulled a knife because he knows what you're capable of . . ."

"I'm so happy that you know everything I did, Sheriff, especially since I can't remember any of it myself." She took a bite of the beans, swallowed hard, and said, "You've got to let me do the cooking around here, Murphy."

"No."

She dropped the corn bread onto the plate and pushed off the cot to return the tray to the floor. "Fine.

I'll starve to death while waiting for my trial." She straightened. "Maybe Todd will bring me something from Marigold's Kitchen."

Murphy met her at the bars. He did not bend to pick up the tray. With hands on hips, he watched her. "Todd cannot afford to buy you anything from Marigold's. He's penniless just like the rest of us in town."

"What are you talking about?"

His gray eyes glittered in the lantern light. "Think about it, Katie. The bank is missing ten thousand dollars. It shut down the day you woke up in Todd's bedroom. It won't reopen until another shipment of cash arrives from Lincoln."

"Well, when will that be?"

He picked up the tray from the floor. "Now you're concerned?"

"Of course."

"Then make it easy. Tell me where you put the money." When she didn't answer, he moved away. "I'll bring you some scrambled eggs in the morning. They're my specialty."

In that moment, Katie knew the sheriff meant to torture her.

On the twelfth night of her incarceration a barroom fight broke out. Katie heard a gunshot and knew the sheriff had stepped off the porch. Quickly, she climbed onto the cot to see what happened. By the time she stood eye level at the window, a man sailed out of the swinging doors of Big Buck's Saloon. He landed in the gravel road and laid there stunned. His hat fluttered out the door behind him and then a huge fellow barreled out the doors holding two men by their shirt collars. He threw them into the dirt near the first man. Katie assumed the large fellow was Big Buck. He was at least forty years old and had manhandled the younger men like rag dolls.

Murphy stood next to Buck and the two of them faced the three men in the street, who swayed like trees in a windstorm. "I want my pistol returned to me," one of them bellowed.

"Go home, Taylor," Buck replied in a booming voice. "Sober up and I'll return your pistol to you."

"I'm not leaving without my gun, you sad old bag of guts," Taylor hollered and staggered toward the steps.

Katie could not hear what the sheriff said, even though she strained further on tiptoe, but whatever it was caused Taylor to reel and glare at Murphy. He said, "I wasn't talking to you, Sheriff. Why don't you go back to that pretty little thing you got locked up over there in that jail?"

A crowd of men and women pushed through the doors of the bar and spilled out onto the walkway. They still held their mugs and whiskey glasses. Everyone laughed when Taylor staggered sideways and nearly fell into the water trough. They laughed harder when Big Buck stepped off the porch and booted Taylor the rest of the way into the trough.

Taylor's friends reacted wildly. One man rushed Buck while the third one tackled the sheriff; they crashed into barrels stacked on the side of the building.

Men and women scattered, drinks spilled; one man grew angry when a bystander jostled him so he punched the fellow in the face. More blows followed and then everyone joined in the fray.

Murphy kicked the drunken man off him and got to his feet. He stood his ground, striking hard as men rushed him. When the sheriff hit a man, that man stayed down. After a while no one had the nerve to come at him anymore. He raised his pistol and shot a bullet skyward.

Everyone paused and stared at Murphy. Even Buck stopped punching the fellow he had by the shirt collar.

"Get out of here," shouted Murphy. When no one moved, the sheriff said in a quieter voice, accompanied by the clicking sound that his pistol made, "I said move. Curfew starts right now. Anyone who sticks around will spend the night in jail."

Men got to their feet and mounted horses; others climbed into sideboard buggies. Buck hit his captive one last time and then let the man fall into the street. When Murphy came into the office again, Katie heard him rummage through his desk. She called, "Are you all right, Sheriff?"

"I'm fine," he said in a low voice. The candle went out and she heard the bench squeak beneath his weight.

"Why didn't you arrest those men?"

"Did you want to spend the night with a bunch of drunks, Miss Thomas?"

The next day Katie thought about Murphy while sitting on the cot, waiting for her lunch. She didn't like him any more than the day she had met him. She still found him arrogant and frustrating, but, if all the madness had not happened, if Katie had simply arrived in town like anybody else, would she have been smitten with Sheriff Wade Murphy? Yes, she definitely would have been, for he was the type of man Katie preferred, one of directness and courage. He feared nothing.

She heard him enter the office, so Katie slid off the cot and approach the bars.

He carried a plate of food in his hands and a glass of tea. "I splurged and bought you meat pie from Marigold's." It was the first she had seen him in the full light of day and he was clean-shaven and wore black from head to boot. He slid the plate beneath the bars.

Katie retrieved it and sat on the cot again to eat. With her fork, she cut into the meat pie. "That is quite a black eye you have, Sheriff."

He fingered the red bruise on his left cheek. "The Benson brothers."

"Who are they?"

"The men Buck threw out of the saloon last night." He continued to stand there and it puzzled Katie. He usually left her alone these days. He said, "I just received a wire from the circuit judge. He'll be delayed a week."

Katie was disappointed and elated at the same time. The delay meant she had to stay in jail another week but it also meant Ben Raines had more time to wake and Katie had longer to remember what happened in the woods two weeks ago. "How's Ben doing?"

"Todd told me he still has an infection. I guess he had a bad night last night, just as you did."

She frowned at him. "Did I?"

"It sounded as though you had a nightmare."

"I don't remember." She took a sip of tea. "What if

Ben wakes today and says I had nothing to do with the robbery?"

"The last time Ben woke he said you had the money." His expression was impersonal, as though he had no interest in pursuing the subject.

"What will you do, Sheriff, when you find out I am innocent of these crimes?"

"That's unlikely."

"I'll be proved innocent," she told him before taking another bite. "And when I am, you'll be sorry that you weren't nicer to me."

"Why will I be sorry, Miss Thomas?"

"You'll be sorry because I'll have nothing to do with you then."

He did not reply and took a step toward the door.

"You're just like Barlett Sanders."

He hesitated. "Barlett Sanders?"

"Mm-hmm. He was a boy at my school who was almost as unpleasant as you are, Sheriff. He and my cousin Nadine were friends, and they both made fun of me because I couldn't read as well as them. They were in the top grade and I was twelve years old."

"Your point?"

"My point is that when Barlett came home from college I'd grown up. Suddenly he wanted me to step out with him but I'd already seen his heart and it was cold and mean. I wouldn't give that man the time of day. *You,* Murphy, are Barlett Sanders."

"Well now, you see, Miss Thomas," he said, pushing the hat off his forehead with his free hand, "there's one big difference between me and Barlett Sanders. Even if you somehow get out of this charge against you, I wouldn't pursue you in any sort of sparking fashion."

That brought her up short. "Why not?"

It was a rare moment when Murphy barked out a laugh. "Because you are a poor reader. If Barlett and Nadine thought so then, I can't step out with you."

His teasing delighted her. It made her feel ordinary again instead of the jailbird she'd become. She countered, "You won't step out with me because I can outshoot you."

"You think just because you can hit a few tin cans in the yard that you can outshoot the sheriff of Victor City?"

She scowled then. "Barlett Sanders."

His smirk turned into a look of confusion.

"He thought he could outshoot me too. I was thirteen the summer before he left for Virginia and he still teased me about being a tomboy. He and his friends, Tucker and Jacob, were in the woods south of town shooting at squirrels and rabbits, and missing everything. I was out there too and trying to stay away from their wild shots. I'd been taking target practice and was walking home. Well, they saw me and started teasing me . . . until we all heard the rattle . . ."

She saw Murphy's interest in the conclusion of her tale but she also knew he would never admit to it. He waited without expression.

Warming to her theme, she dropped her voice in a melodramatic storytelling tone. "It was striking distance to Barlett's face as it sat upon one of the mulberry bushes."

"The snake was on top of the bush?"

"Yes, it was. Barlett turned around to shoot it but he got so upset that he dropped his rifle. The snake positioned itself to strike but I had it in my sights and shot the head clean off of it."

"You did not."

"Run over there and ask Todd if I didn't."

"Todd wasn't there."

"No, but Jacob Levee went back to Newville and told everybody he ran into what had happened. I always liked that Jacob Levee."

"Well there again, Miss Thomas, I'm no Barlett Sanders. I've never backed down from a snake yet."

"Yes, but you'd miss," she told him, hoping to keep the conversation going.

"I'll bring you dinner at the usual time."

"Who was the fellow who rode into town today?"

The sheriff stopped at the door. "Which one? There's a stock sale going on."

"He was too far down the road for me to see him well but he didn't look like a cattleman."

With his hand on the knob, he told her, "I know what's wrong, Miss Thomas. You're bored. It happens every time I jail someone for more than a couple of days. You start to see things. You pay too much attention to what's happening out on the street."

"All right," she told him, patting her lips with the napkin. "He just looked different from the rest of the people who come through here."

"How was he different?"

"He dressed like a city slicker."

"It's not against the law to dress up," he told her and stepped out of the room.

He did not think of his conversation with Katie until later in the evening. Murphy supposed she was right. Most people in town did not dress like city folks. Usually when a stranger came to town done up, he was a high-stakes gambler. Murphy would not tolerate gamblers in Victor City. He moved along the deserted boardwalk, past the mill, the post office, and Marigold's Kitchen. Few lamps lit the businesses that closed at candle lighting. Most of the town's activity came from the saloon. He crossed the wide road. As he drew closer to the bar, he heard men talking, women laughing, and the bartender's rich baritone shouting over the other voices in the room. Buck laughed about something and when Murphy came through the doors, the big man turned to greet him. "Heya, Sheriff."

Buck was one of the original settlers in Victor City. The stage depot workers swore the saloon was already standing when they sawed logs for the first building. *He came out of the wilderness,* they said. *He is a gypsy,* others claimed. Murphy had never heard a straight story yet from the bartender regarding where he hailed from and as far as being a gypsy. Murphy believed he might be, for Maurice "Big Buck" Lamar was olive-hued, black-eyed, and the hair left on his head was raven black. His nose dominated his face, unless he smiled, and then his two front teeth stuck out the most. He ran a clean bar with no swindling card games, disorderly conduct, or prostitution. A businessman such as Buck made Murphy's job a lot easier. Buck served liquor, lawfully so, and made it an art by serving the fanciest concoctions this side of the Mississippi. Tall Terror and Absolute Apricot Shot were among the local favorites besides plain beer and straight whiskey. His latest blends and fusions included Coconut Clock, High Drunken Shandy, and Rotten Squirt. Big Buck was as much of an alchemist as Dr. Todd Thomas was.

"Heya," Murphy replied and stood at one end of the long and polished bar. Nearly fifty patrons filled the room. Murphy recognized most of the men. "Has Taylor returned for his gun?"

"Naw," Buck growled. "Sobered up. That boy is too cowardly to come back to see me. He'll send his daddy to fetch it for him."

"Give the pistol to me," Murphy instructed. "I'll keep it in the office. If Taylor's father comes looking for it, send him to me."

"Pleasure," Buck said, grinning and reaching beneath the bar. "That old man will soak his chaps if he has to talk to you about his rowdy boy."

Murphy kept his eyes on the crowd. Few men sat at the bar, more reclined at the gaming tables. "Anybody in here you don't know?"

The skin beneath Buck's jaw jiggled. "Every fella here is my best friend as long as I pour the whiskey."

"Newcomers?"

Buck thought for a moment and then sat Taylor's pistol on the bar. "A pretty man has been visiting for the past couple of nights. Garcia is the name he gave me. I watched him at first to make sure he wasn't cheatin' but he stays real quiet and leaves early."

"Is he here now?"

"Yup, he came in a couple of minutes ago. He's sitting at the far table by the alley door."

Thick carpet covered half the floor where marble game tables set. Alabaster figurines had their place in each corner. A large gilded mirror hung behind the bar and velvet drapes kept the lights low.

Three men sat at the last table playing cards. Kent, Elliot, and John hooted over some joke as Murphy made his way toward them. "Evening," he greeted.

"Evening, Sheriff," came their general salute. "How about a hand, Murphy? Got a couple of dollars to lose?"

"Too much hard luck in my life right now. I'm looking for a fellow named Garcia. Have you seen him?"

Kent answered, "He just left. He sat at the table to play but got up quick-like a few moments ago."

Murphy saw that the alley door stood open. "What does Garcia look like?"

The three men glanced at each other. Elliot said, "About your height, Sheriff, but he is wiry built and severe-looking."

John nodded. "Well dressed too; he wears one of those fancy vests of quilted material."

"It's called brocade," Kent corrected.

John stared at Kent. "What are you, some kind of poesy who knows how to measure and sew?"

Murphy did not stay to hear the end of their discussion. Assuming Garcia went out the alley door, Murphy moved that way. He did not have a torch and the back street was too dark to track prints. He drew his pistol, working on a hunch. He stepped quietly from the saloon and then walked behind Blue Bells. He tried the door but it remained locked. Walking farther, he saw lights in the dressmaker's store.

Katie dozed. She would sleep more peacefully when Murphy slept on the bench. She heard footsteps and thought he had returned, but then she realized that the noise did not come from the outer office, it came from outside her window. Since Murphy never returned to the office on this side of the building, Katie sat up to listen. She swung her feet to the floor.

"Katie?"

Staring at the window, she did not reply. The only light in the room came from a lamp in the outer office. When she peered at the window again she saw gloved hands gripping the bars.

She scrambled off the cot and backed away.

The whisper sounded like a growl, "Katie!"

The front door to the office closed loudly and relief surged through her. She twisted around and called, "Sheriff?"

Something heavy landed on his desk and a moment later Murphy walked into the jail room carrying a lantern. He hung it on the wall.

Katie glanced at the window again. The gloved hands had disappeared.

Murphy did not seem to notice her alarm. "Do you know anyone named Garcia?" He adjusted the wick and then came to stand in front of her. His presence, even aggressive, offered some comfort.

"I don't know anyone named Garcia."

Murphy tilted his head, thinking. Crossing his arms over his chest, he said, "About my height, wears fancy clothing . . . he looks stern."

"Does he wear black gloves?" She studied at the window again. "Someone walked past and grabbed the bars."

Murphy took the lantern off the wall and stepped out of the room. Katie heard his boots crunching in the rocks and she stood on the bench to peek down at him. She saw the soft glow of the flame in the lantern and saw the top of Murphy's hat as he bent to study the ground. "What do you see?"

"Gravel."

Katie sat on the bench again. When Murphy came into the room, he had softened a bit. "You're frightened?"

"Whoever it was knew me because he whispered my name."

"He spoke your name?"

She nodded. "Where are you going?"

She must have sounded anxious because he called over his shoulder. "I'll get Todd to stay with you."

"Someone stood at your window? Who? How did he know your name?"

"Stop it, Todd. If anyone is going to get into a dither, let it be me." She sat on the bench and pulled her knees to her chest. "Maybe I dreamed it."

"You have the sheriff searching the town because you dreamed someone called your name?" Her brother stood there looking disheveled with his hair lying over to the side and his spectacles halfway down his nose. He said, "No wonder he finds you so irritating."

"He said that?"

"He doesn't have to. Murphy is always riled these days. His bad mood started the day you came to town." Todd did not look at her any longer but at the chair in the corner of the room. He dragged it to the bars and sat. "You have the same effect on me."

"You've been in a bad mood since you were five years old," she countered.

"The day you were born, I remember."

"What are you mad about? Did Murphy pull you out of bed?"

"No, I was up. Ben Raines is awake."

Katie slid off the cot and rushed toward the bars. "What did he say?"

"Muttered and confused talk, mostly. He needs time I suppose."

"Time? I could get the black gown while he sleeps in your spare bedroom."

"You won't hang. Eventually Ben will set the story straight." Todd pushed at his glasses. "You might show patience with the man. He nearly died trying to save your life."

"He didn't try to save my life."

"What?"

"Once the gunfire started, he pushed the horses too hard. Obviously he knew they were about to get robbed."

Todd rose slowly from his chair. "You remember that?"

Katie lifted her shoulder. "How else would the coach tip over unless the horses raced up the hill sideways?" She just talked, not recalling a memory exactly, just facts.

"Did Murphy tell you the stage tipped?" When she shrugged, Todd pressed her, "The stage went up the hill sideways?"

"Yes, I stood there and watched it."

"You stood . . . ?"

"What's wrong with you, Todd? Everyone is upset about the stage robbery. These aren't new facts."

"Everyone is upset about the holdup, yes, and about the fact that we buried four people last week. And frankly, it sounds like you had something to do with it!"

He certainly knew how to sum up the problem. Katie did not mean to snap his head off when she said, "Why don't you go home, Todd?" Sometimes the circumstance closed in on her. Todd left the room looking hurt and confused. After a few moments, she hollered out the window to him, "I love you!"

"I'm flattered," Murphy told her, coming into the room.

"I yelled to Todd."

"Todd's not here." Looking smug, he approached the bars.

Her head started to throb and she did not attempt to argue. Instead, she slumped onto the cot and found her pillow.

Murphy did not move away but studied her. "Are you ill?"

"No," she answered, rubbing her forehead. "I just don't want to talk to you."

"Why not?"

She watched him. The lantern on the wall threw off a golden light that softened his features. She doubted it softened his temperament, however. In the subtle light his pale eyes appeared darker blue and he watched her now as she watched him, intently and curiously. "What would we talk about, Sheriff? You don't believe anything I tell you."

"I don't remember you ever trying to convince me of anything. When I ask you a question you either say you don't remember or it's none of my business."

"When did I say . . . ?"

"Anthony Ricci."

She gave a soft laugh and shook her head. "You wouldn't try to understand. You'd only scoff at me and call me a liar."

"Why don't you give it a try?"

"No."

He took a step, pulled the chair from the corner, and straddled it backward.

"Come on, Miss Thomas, here's your chance. I'll listen intently and I won't call you a liar."

She did not reply and leaned her head against the wall to shut her eyes. Maybe if she ignored him, he would leave her alone.

"How did you get acquainted with him? Did you meet him at your aunt's house as she claimed you did? Was it love at first sight?"

Katie opened her eyes to frown at him.

"No?" He pushed the Stetson back off his forehead. "A chance meeting in the night, then?"

"He came to dinner."

"Dinner? So you flirted with him when your cousin's back was turned?"

"No, I watched him." She kept her eyes mostly closed so that she could see Murphy's reaction through her lashes. "His voice was the most unusual that I'd ever heard. It was low sounding and raspy and it fascinated me until I actually heard what he said."

"What do you mean?"

"I thought it was strange the way he spoke to my aunt."

"What way was that?"

Katie rubbed her eyes. "Mischievously." The image was still strong in her mind. Aunt Victoria had kept an elegant dining room. Candles lit the space from above, making the crystal sparkle. Anthony had sat on her right side, at one end of the table, and her aunt sat on Katie's left at the other end of the table.

Victoria, at fifty, kept up her appearance. She'd dyed her hair black and always painted her face carefully. She wore a scarlet dress that evening with a low-fitting bodice that showed deep cleavage. Anthony's eyes traveled there often.

Katie fluffed her pillow without looking at Murphy. "They acted as though they liked each other."

"What did your cousin think about that?"

"Nadine didn't notice. When she'd turn away, Anthony smiled at my aunt and raised his brow as though they shared a private joke."

"You think they had an affair?"

It was odd how Murphy's voice lulled Katie. Her headache subsided and she answered, "When Anthony left for the evening, he opened the door for Nadine to step outside. They were going to say good night, I suppose, but before he walked out the door I saw my aunt slip something into his hand."

"A note?"

"Money."

"Why would she do that?"

Katie found her blanket on the end of the bed and pulled it over her legs. "I don't know, but I thought she gave him money to take Nadine somewhere. It didn't make sense. Nadine bragged about how wealthy Anthony was and said he owned two or three businesses."

"When did that take place?" Murphy asked her. "Todd didn't know about your relationship with Ricci until last spring."

"December of last year when I was home for the holiday. Nadine thought Anthony would propose to her at Christmas. She really thought he loved her." She lay on her side and pulled the blanket over her shoulder.

"He didn't love her?" He sounded genuinely interested. Did he believe her?

"He couldn't have loved her because the next day he came to call, Nadine and my aunt had gone out. He knew they wouldn't be there; they'd discussed it at dinner. But he came to the house and wanted to speak to me. He wanted to get to know me, he said." She pictured it again in her mind. There stood Anthony in the keeping room, tall, elegant, and black-haired. Many women found him attractive, but Katie did not. He had a look about him that was hungry, as though he could devour a person in one bite, and if there was a theatrical production that needed Satan, Anthony would fit the bill. He had the blackest eyes she had ever seen. It was as though he had no pupils, only bottomless, soulless eyes. "He made me uneasy," she told Murphy. "He sat close on the settee and he kept . . ."

When she did not finish the sentence, Murphy prompted, "What?"

"I asked him to leave."

"Did he?"

"Yes, and he ran straight to Nadine to claim that I'd flirted shamelessly with him and that he barely escaped my clutches. Of course Nadine flew into a rage and confronted me. Aunt Victoria took her side. She said I always stole Nadine's boyfriends. Aunt Victoria is a stern woman, serious-minded, and sometimes cold-natured. When Todd and I arrived to live with her I was a bit of a live coal . . ." She smiled at Murphy after she said it.

"That's hard to believe."

Katie laughed softly. "Anyway, Anthony became insufferable after that. If we were all in a room together he would say, 'Is something wrong, Katie? Why are you staring at me?' I never stared at him. I avoided him. He said it to make Nadine angry with me. Anthony likes to play games. Then, one day after Christmas, I visited my girlfriend Lenora in Newville, north of Springfield. She'd just married and I wanted to see their home. We walked into the front room together and who do you think walked by her front window?"

"Ricci?"

"Correct, and immediately I thought that he'd followed me but he crossed the road and knocked on a neighbor's door. Lenora and I pressed our noses to her window and when the door opened, I saw an older woman answer. Just before the door closed, Anthony embraced her. I was ready to leave an hour later and the woman's door opened again. Out strolled Anthony. His shirt hung out his pants and he adjusted his coat."

"Did you tell Nadine about it?"

Katie shook her head on the pillow and whispered, "I followed him."

"Alone?"

"I put on my heavy coat and scarf and wrapped the scarf so that it covered my face. Then I followed him to the old part of town."

"That was unwise."

She nodded. "It was stupid. We call it Old Town and it's not a nice place. Anthony met with all different sorts of people: men, women, some high-toned, and some not. He slipped cash to several people and took some from others. Then he went into a tall house on a corner. It looked nice considering the area. I'd just decided to leave because two men kept watching me. But just before I turned, I heard a blood-curdling scream. It cut off quickly but it came from the house that Anthony had gone into."

"And you, what, went and peered into the window?"

She ignored his sarcasm. "I left. In a hurry."

"Did he find out that you'd followed him?"

"Yes. I don't know if he saw me or if someone told him that I followed him."

"What did he do?"

Katie had grown sleepy but in that instant she remembered how sharply fearful things had turned out that evening. "He came to dinner."

When she stayed silent over long, Murphy asked, "Did he accuse you to your family?"

"No, he acted as though nothing bothered him. The only strange thing he said was that he wanted to spend the night. I thought it was a strange request. I thought he would have his own home. But my cousin and my aunt were happy to have him and prepared the guest room for him."

Murphy waited for her to go on, staring at her curiously. Did he believe her?

"I went to bed," she whispered.

"And that was it?"

"No."

Murphy's brow lifted in question.

"After midnight I woke up. Someone had sat on my bed. I started to cry out but Anthony slapped his hand over my mouth. He laid beside me, to scare me, and he said, 'If you wanted to go to Old Town, you could've asked me. I would've shown you around.' I was so scared that I could barely breathe. Then he said, 'If you follow me again or if you tell Nadine or Victoria what you saw, I will drag you to Old Town and you will spend the rest of your life working for me.'"

"What did he mean? Prostitution?"

She shrugged.

"Did he hurt you?"

"He left the room."

Murphy's brows gathered. "And your aunt saw him leave? That was what the telegraph said."

"I'd never heard that until you read it." She yawned. "Can we talk about this later, Sheriff? I'm very sleepy."

He returned the chair into the corner and shut the door on his way out. Was Katie telling the truth? He sat behind his desk and ran through her story again in his mind. If she told the truth about her relationship with Ricci, did it matter? It did not shed new light on the stagecoach robbery. However, it did shed new light on Katie Thomas' character. She was impulsive, reckless in her actions, but she had not acted criminally.

Murphy tipped the chair and rocked a minute. If she did not have a relationship with Anthony Ricci then she was not necessarily lying about everything else.

He righted his chair with some noise. Tossing the Stetson onto the rack, he stepped outside into the yard. The night air felt cool. September was on them and it would not be long before the days turned cold.

He was not wrong about Katie! He had never been wrong when working a hunch; he prided himself on that.

Why did the headmistress in Chicago believe Katie and Anthony kept company and were stepping out together? How was that possible? It meant that Mrs. Volker was a witness. It meant that Katie playacted a part in front of him.

He felt a brief moment of relief and sat on the step. The girl had yet to be straightforward with him. She had been evasive, stubborn, and rebellious; she had gone into Ben's room; she left town; she would not answer his questions.

Agitated, Murphy stood again. If Katie didn't shoot the man in the woods, then who did? No one else was around. And if she shot him, then she shot Ben, Theodore Moon, and Caldwell, and that was the tale of the bullets. Katie Thomas was guilty, so why was his instinct telling him to investigate further? This was an old story now, wasn't it?

Chapter Five

Murphy stood at the bars when Katie woke the next morning. "You're getting lazy," he told her. "I've already done a turn around the town."

Katie saw the shadows on the ceiling and rolled to a sitting position. She had dreamed all night that someone had been chasing her. She sat on the edge of the cot, rubbed her eyes, and patted her bumpy hair. Curls stuck out in every direction.

"Do you want to bathe and change your clothes?"

Katie looked at him while waiting for his words to make sense. She had a hard time waking and it caused her stomach to hurt. After he unlocked the cell, she followed him to the outer office. Her Saratoga trunk sat in the corner. Todd had brought it over the day after her arrest. Now she knelt to sift through the clothing. She selected a camisole, underpants; she sensed the sheriff's eyes on her and she turned to look at him.

He leaned against the wall to watch her. He folded his arms and crossed one boot over the other.

"Do you mind?" she asked, holding her underclothes beneath the rim of the trunk so that he could not see them.

He frowned, pushed off the wall, and busied himself at the desk.

Katie selected soft deerskin pants and a long-sleeved white blouse. She lifted her leather boots from the side of the trunk.

Murphy handed her a paper sack when she got to her feet. From the top drawer, he pulled a pair of steel cuffs. "Hold out your hands."

She sighed as she did so. It was hard to maintain any sort of dignity when paraded through town with cuff chains tinkling. Murphy said, "We'll take the alley."

The sun was bright in a dark blue sky and a light breeze came off the mountains from the south. Red painted the leaves on the maple trees behind Marigold's, a few sprinkles of yellow touched them too.

When they reached the bathhouse, Murphy held up his finger indicating that Katie stay put, and she lethargically turned from him to gaze at the street. The tenement house was a busy spot this morning. The man who owned the establishment stood on the walk and shouted directions to the two men above him working to hang a new sign from the second story. *Blue Bells, established 1868.* So the place was fairly new, Katie reckoned. The whole town was no more than eight to ten years old, and it was a peaceful spot to live. She glanced northward and saw the Platte in the distance.

Someone would think to put a railroad through sometime and more people would learn of the tranquility here.

Murphy knocked on the door again and when no one answered, he opened it. "Katie." He motioned her inside. "We'll have to wait."

Katie loved bathhouses. This one was remarkably feminine with rose print wallpaper and colorful paintings scattered around the room. Perfumed soap invited women to soak long. Bottles of toilet water and colored salts lined the counter. Two tubs sat in the back area.

Murphy looked completely out of place. He had removed his hat and twisted it in his hand. Finally, he sat in the wooden chair by the door. He motioned for her to have a seat.

Sitting next to him, she remained quiet. The headache she had last night left her dopey. Murphy said something and Katie turned to him. "I'm sorry, what?"

"I said I didn't understand something about what you told me last night regarding your relationship with Anthony Ricci." When she did not reply, he said, "All of it took place in Springfield, right? How did the headmistress in Chicago know about your relationship?"

She leaned back in her chair and stared at her fingers. She toyed with the cuff chain. "Because Anthony was in Chicago."

"To see you?"

"No," she replied with a small laugh. "My roommate Rosemarie and I had been ice-skating. We walked home and were distracted by the five-and-dime sale, and while Rosemarie studied a gadget, I think it was a coin keeper, I gazed out the window. I thought I saw Anthony. The man looked like him but I wasn't sure. He walked into a tobacco store and I saw him just inside. Rosemarie asked me what was wrong because I must have gone stiff standing there."

Murphy sat shoulder to shoulder with her and she glanced at him. He asked, "Did you tell her then what happened?"

"I'd already told her what happened. All I had to say was 'it's Anthony' and she nearly dropped her skates."

"So what did you do?"

"We followed him."

"Katie, for crying out loud!" Murphy no longer watched her and put his head against the wall.

"I know," she placated quickly. "But I felt much safer in Chicago. He couldn't threaten me there. I lived at the college. He couldn't get inside."

Did he believe her? She felt nearly hopeful.

He still had his head on the wall but now he frowned at her. "You are impetuous. You've already proven that a couple of times here too."

"Do you want me to go on or do you want to yell at me some more?"

"I might want to yell at you some more."

Katie played with the cuff chain again.

"All right, go on."

She offered a faint smile. "We followed him to Charling Street, but we kept a safe distance."

"I'll bet."

"He met a man there." Suddenly her headache came back and she rubbed her brow.

Murphy asked, "What man?"

"Pardon?"

"You said he met—"

"Charting Street, that's right. It was number 12. He went inside for a time."

"What about the man he met?"

Katie watched Murphy again. His features showed concern. "What man? Stop interrupting the story, Murphy."

"Sorry." He did not look sorry. He appeared troubled.

She went on, slowly at first, watching Murphy's expression. "We left quickly. I didn't necessarily want to provoke any more problems, so we went back to school—after ice cream. He was there."

"At the ice-cream shop?"

"No, at the college. He was in Mrs. Barnes' office. He requested permission to see me and told the headmistress that my relationship with Nadine was strained but that he wanted to inform me of their engagement. Mrs. Barnes closed the door to give us privacy."

"He threatened you?"

She nodded.

"He'd seen you?"

"Yes."

"What did he say?"

"I can't tell you." It was not as though she did not want to tell the sheriff the truth, but it embarrassed her how Anthony had spoken to her. He had made repulsive suggestions, suggestions of what he would do to her if she ever told anybody where he was that day.

Thankfully, Murphy did not press the point. For the

first time he did not accuse her of hiding something from him. Perhaps he sensed what Anthony said to her because he asked, "He scared you?"

"Yes, very much so, and he told me that the college building wouldn't protect me. If I ran, he'd find me."

"Did you go to Mrs. Barnes?"

She shook her head and whispered, "I was too scared."

"So you let him manipulate you?"

Katie looked him in the eye. "No, Sheriff, I didn't. Rosemarie's uncle is a police officer."

Murphy relaxed then. What was he angry about, her stupidity? "Good," he said. "So you told the officer about it?"

"I did. He started an investigation, but in the meanwhile, Anthony liked his game of frightening me. Everywhere I went, he was there. He didn't always speak to me, but he showed up at the skating pond and in shops I went into. Some of the girls from school noticed him. A couple of them asked me about him and gushed on about how attractive he was and what a seductive voice he had. One girl, Betsy Bach, approached Anthony and flirted with him. We didn't get along well, Betsy and I, but I felt a need to warn her to leave the man alone and to warn her that he was dangerous."

"She thought you were jealous?"

He believed her! Katie saw that Murphy believed her story and that he understood Betsy Bach's reaction. She smiled at him.

"I am a student of behavior, remember? Or I always thought I was, anyway. So what happened?"

"Betsy went to Mrs. Barnes and told her that she saw me with Anthony, and without asking my side of it, Mrs. Barnes called my Aunt Victoria and they confronted me regarding my disreputable behavior. I denied seeing Anthony but my aunt started to cry and claimed Nadine's heart would be broken. I was placed on probation and wasn't allowed to leave the college."

Murphy twisted to see her better. "But you did, you sneaked out after dark."

"I did, but not to see Anthony. Rosemarie told me that her uncle, Sergeant Leonard, wanted to speak to me. I met with him and he asked me again about where Anthony went that day in Chicago, the day we followed him. I repeated number 12 Charling, and he asked me who was with Anthony."

"The man you spoke about?"

She frowned at him. "Sergeant Leonard asked me if I would testify that I saw him and Hank Walker at 12 Charling around two thirty."

"Hank Walker?"

She ignored his constant interruptions. "I said that I would and I did testify and now Anthony is in jail in New York for the attempted murder of Elizabeth Harding of number 12 Charling Street."

"That was why you didn't want to go to New York."

His question confused Katie.

His eyes watched her closely. "The first day I spoke to you, you said, 'Obviously I didn't want to go to New York.'"

"Right. You have a good memory, Sheriff."

The door opened and an auburn-haired woman stepped into the bathhouse. She was in her thirties, Katie guessed, and was a tall elegant woman. She acted surprised to see them and then apologized twice for running an errand.

Murphy said, "It's fine, Hazel. We didn't wait long." He stepped toward the door and without so much as a good-bye, he said, "I'll be back in an hour. I have to send a telegram."

After bringing Katie her lunch, Murphy left the office for the rest of the day. He did not return at dinner and Todd brought her food at six o'clock. "What's the sheriff up to?" she asked when Todd took the tray.

"I don't know but he's working on something. He didn't even ask about Ben Raines when he stopped by."

Later in the evening, the door between the office and the jail opened and Murphy stepped toward the bars. He took the keys off the wall and unlocked the cell door. "Come with me." When she did not move fast enough, he repeated, "Come with me now." He kept his voice a whisper and there was such urgency to it that Katie jumped off the cot and rushed toward him. His eyes glanced over her. "I need to cover your hair." He led Katie into the office and pulled the blanket off his own cot. "Fit this over your head."

The sheriff led her out the back door and when they stood in the yard, Murphy instructed, "Don't make a sound. Don't call out." He pulled a pistol from his belt, glanced left and right, and then directed her into the alley.

No lanterns lit the alleyway. No candles flamed inside

the closed businesses. She only heard their footsteps and a note or two from Big Buck's piano across the road.

Her cape slipped. Murphy grabbed the fabric to keep it in place. In the pale moon's light, his face looked set for danger. He pushed her toward the street without a word.

Buck met them at the back door of his supply room. He took Katie's wrists and without acknowledging her, he nodded to Murphy.

"Keep her out of sight until you hear from me." He did not look at her again and left the doorway.

She had only seen Buck from a distance and although she knew he was *Big* Buck, she was still surprised at his height. He was at least a foot and a half taller than Katie was and outweighed her five times over. He pulled her toward the back of the room near a desk. Crates of liquor lined one wall to the ceiling and it was between an opening there that Buck directed her.

She stopped and backed away to face him. "Why did the sheriff bring me here?"

The man's broad nose wrinkled and he folded his massive arms over his chest. "He's trying to save you, girly, and he knows I am the man to protect you. Now step between them boxes and crouch down."

"But where is Murphy going?"

"Garcia is back. The sheriff got a good look at him and recognized him from a handbill. He said the man's name ain't Garcia, it's Richie or Ricky or some such name." Buck grabbed a huge gun from the corner and checked the barrels. "He thinks Richie will try to break you out of jail, but that'll be a mistake. The sheriff's waiting for him."

Katie's chest tightened. Who was Richie? Did Buck mean Ricci? But that was not possible; Anthony was in prison in New York. Even if he got out, he would not know Katie was in Victor City. Unless . . . Rosemarie!

Minutes dragged.

Murphy sat behind his desk, slipped a derringer up his sleeve, and shoved a knife into his boot. He had left the door to his office opened.

Footsteps crunched through the gravel at the side of the building and then boots stomped onto the walk. Two long shadows appeared in the doorway. Anthony Ricci walked into the room followed by the man who had threatened Barney in the woods; he still wore a sling over his shoulder. His clothes were filthy and grime covered his hands.

Ricci, however, appeared elegant in a silver and black vest. A double holster fell across his hips. Pearl-handled grips protruded from the belt. Though he was a handsome man, Anthony Ricci looked thin, cruel, and hungry to kill. He pulled one of the pistols from the holster but tempered the action by taking off his hat in a polite gesture. "Evening, Sheriff," he offered in a deep tone.

Murphy pushed to his feet while fingering his own weapon.

"Don't try it," Ricci warned. "I can easily take you." He cocked the weapon. The other fellow closed the door.

Anthony motioned toward his companion. "I believe you've met Jake Cherry."

Jake showed an oily grin. "You ought to know the man's name that's here to kill you."

"Not now," Anthony told him, still smiling. "I think you know who I am, Sheriff."

"Garcia?"

He laughed and the sound of it boomed like thunder. "You're not as good a lawman as everyone thinks you are."

"What can I do for you?" Murphy asked, stepping out from behind the desk.

Jake Cherry spit on the floor. "You can go straight to hell."

Anthony's smile withered. "Show some restraint, Jake. You'll get your chance soon enough." To Murphy he said, "I'm here to see one of your prisoners."

"You don't need a gun to visit a prisoner." He walked toward the cell room door and stood in front of it.

Ricci's eyes followed his movement. "Somehow I didn't think you'd unlock the door and let me take her with me."

"I thought you said you wanted to visit her."

"You thought wrong."

"What would a man like you want with Mary? She's a simple pickpocket."

Ricci's brow rose. "Mary?"

"Aren't you here to see Mary Billingsworth, or did you get more than your own name wrong, *Anthony*?"

Ricci threw back his head and laughed. "Now this is what I expected from you, Sheriff. Jake, the man knows how to play the game."

"I don't play games." Jerking his arm slightly, Murphy

pulled the derringer from his shirtsleeve and pointed the small pistol at the other man's face.

Ricci's black eyes danced in the lantern light and in a magnanimous gesture, he threw out his arms. "Shoot away, Sheriff. It may be your only chance."

Murphy cocked the gun. "Drop your weapon."

Jake Cherry pulled a long knife out of the back of his belt. The blade flashed like the head of a rattlesnake and Murphy ducked. The knife impaled the door behind him. As Murphy ducked, Ricci kicked him in the face and the derringer clattered across the wood floor. Blood poured form Murphy's nose.

Ricci hunkered down next to him. "Now, you see there, you've upset me."

Murphy brought his fist around and punched Ricci hard on the jaw.

The man fell backward but jumped to his feet to stomp Murphy in the ribs. "GET UP."

Murphy tripped Ricci behind the knees, sending him to the floor.

They both scrambled for their guns.

Jake pulled his small pistol and pointed it at Murphy. "Let me shoot him."

"No," Anthony shouted, coming to his feet with his gun in hand. He grabbed Murphy by the back of the shirt to haul him to his feet. "Put your hands behind your head."

Jake Cherry opened the cell door. "I found her. She's in here."

Ricci shoved Murphy toward the door and then toward the cell.

The seamstress got to her feet and walked carefully, hiding a gun that Murphy had given her in the folds of her skirt.

"Who are you?" Anthony demanded.

"Mary."

Jake Cherry studied her. "This ain't the girl I saw in the woods the other day."

Ricci pushed Murphy against the bars and then spun him around. "Where's Katie?"

"Who's Katie?"

"I saw her with you, Sheriff. I saw Katie Thomas walking with you today. Where did you take her?"

"I told you—"

"Liar." Bits of spittle flew from Ricci's lips. He pointed the gun straight at Mary. "If you don't tell me where you took her, I'll shoot this impostor, and then I'll shoot you." He stepped up to Murphy and came nose to nose with him. "Then who will protect your town, Sheriff, while I kill everyone I see until I find Katie?"

Mary lifted the pistol and pulled the trigger. The bullet exploded into the wall next to Ricci's face. Jake Cherry ran from the room but Anthony shoved Murphy hard enough that they both fell to the floor.

Mary trained the pistol on both men. "STOP!"

Murphy pushed Ricci off him and grabbed the knife in his boot. He hurled it hard. The knife planted deeply into Ricci's thigh just as Ricci's pistol exploded.

A bullet ripped into Murphy's chest . . . lights dimmed . . . he heard Mary scream and then scream again. Everything went black.

* * *

Katie heard the outcries and the gunshots. Buck pushed off the desk and bolted toward the door. "Everybody is heading toward Murphy's place," he hollered over his shoulder. "Get between them boxes."

"I don't think we're safe here. What if something happens to Murphy?"

The bartender spun around. "We're not going anywhere. Don't you run into that barroom." He reached the door before Katie did and slammed and locked it. "You don't have to be scared, girly. I told you I'd protect you. Now get into that hole." He directed her toward it and nearly stuffed her inside. "If Garcia comes here, he'll get nothing but a belly full of lead." He tucked the buffalo gun beneath his arm and walked out onto the stoop.

Terror made her tremble enough that the bottles inside the crates knocked together. She would suffocate here! Katie squeezed outside the boxes and watched Buck from behind. She would make a run for it if she saw Anthony Ricci. No locked door would stop her. She would run right through it carrying the knob with her.

Five minutes went by. The piano music had died as the patrons rushed toward the sheriff's office. Buck turned around to step into the supply room again. "What did I tell you, girly?" he said, angry now. "You get back in there."

Anthony Ricci slipped through the door behind him, grabbed a chair from the corner, and smashed it across Buck's shoulders.

"Buck!" Katie screamed, but too late. The big man

went down with a thud and his rifle clattered across the floor.

Ricci smiled at Katie.

"How did you know to find her in here?" his companion asked. Katie recognized him at once.

Nodding at Buck, he answered, "He was the only person not running toward the jailhouse." He stepped around the bartender and moved toward Katie.

Through a gray fog, Murphy heard Todd's voice and felt the doctor touch his head, neck, and chest. When Todd tore open Murphy's shirt, a searing pain sent Murphy into a sitting position.

The shock of the sheriff's sudden movement sent Todd scrambling backward. Then he grabbed Murphy by the shoulders and pushed him backward again. "Stay still, let me look at you."

"He's alive," someone shouted from the doorway.

Todd glanced at Mary, out of the cell now, and still holding the six-shooter. "Get everyone out of here," he told her.

Murphy got one hand on the bars to pull upward.

"I need to finish examining you. You're bleeding. I need to sew you up."

"Stop," Murphy insisted. "Just bandage it."

"It's a deep slice on your left side, Murphy. There's no bullet but you'll need stitches . . ."

"I said wrap it. You can stitch it later."

For a moment, they glared at each other and then Todd grabbed alcohol from his bag, poured it on a small cloth, and pressed it to the wound.

Murphy came off the floor gritting his teeth. "What is wrong with you?"

Todd narrowed his eyes. Between clenched lips he said, "I don't want you to get an infection."

Murphy pulled away, frowning at him, but all Todd had in his hand was gauze and a bandage now. "I thought you were my friend and now you're trying to kill me?"

"Shut up and let me wrap it. You're the worst patient I've ever had. Sarah Crowe didn't bellyache so much."

Murphy got to his feet and finished the wrapping himself.

"Let me look the back of your head. You must've hit it hard on the chair. You're bleeding there too . . . Where is Katie?"

Murphy buttoned his shirt. "She's with Buck."

Half a dozen people still stood in the outer office. "Get home," Murphy told them. "Arm yourselves. A killer is walking the streets." He grabbed his rifle, two pistols, and replaced the knife in his boot.

Buck struggled to sit when Murphy and Todd entered the stockroom. He had his hand on the back of his neck and rubbed it hard. Murphy kneeled next to him but his eyes scanned the room. "What happened?"

"Near as I can tell, I got hit with that chair." He nodded at the broken wood scattered on the floor.

Murphy and Todd helped him to his feet. "Where's Katie?"

Buck would not look at the sheriff but studied the floor instead. "I couldn't stop him. I saw him grab her just before everything went black. She tried to get out the barroom door."

"Who took her?" Todd asked, wild-eyed now. "Who took Katie?"

Murphy asked Buck, "Do you still have your rifle?"

The bartender walked around Murphy and snatched the gun from the floor. "No one touches Petunia but me."

Murphy eyed Todd, wondering how much help the doctor would be in such an agitated state. "Do you have someone to watch Ben?"

"I don't know, Mary I guess, but Murphy . . ."

"I deputize you both in the name of the law."

Buck raised his chin and his right hand in a solemn oath. Todd stared between the bartender and the sheriff, pale-faced and panicked.

"I swear you in by the authority granted me by Logan County. I form this posse to track, apprehend, and, if necessary, shoot to kill Jake Cherry and Anthony Ricci."

Todd exploded, "Anthony Ricci?!"

"Keep a hold on him," Murphy told Buck.

"Forget Ricci, I'm going to kill Katie. I'm going to peel her hide and . . ."

Chapter Six

Ricci held tight to Katie as they rode across an open meadow in the dark countryside. The horse snorted disapproval when Ricci kicked its sides continually. Katie knew that the sheriff had wounded Ricci. Blood soaked through his pant leg and even stained the side of her clothing. She assumed he had shot the sheriff, for Katie had heard the cries when Ricci pulled her through the alleyway. Was Murphy dead? She refused to believe that. Murphy would not die, he was too mulish and forceful and vigorous to die. And, if he did die, who would rescue her?

Todd would try. As much as she loved him, Katie did not put much stock in her brother's ability to track Ricci, rescue her, and keep alive himself all at the same time.

Moonlight hit the water and Ricci reined in. He slid from the horse and balanced painfully on one leg for a moment. Then he held his hand out for Katie to dismount. He was always a gentleman, Ricci was, a criminal bon vivant and man about the theater. If he dropped the reins, she would tear off into the night. She did not care if one of them shot her in the back. She knew heaven was a far better place than the one Ricci had in mind for her.

Sensing her intentions, Ricci grabbed her around the waist and pulled her down beside him. His features appeared wolfish in the moonlight. "Do you think you can escape me, Katie?" He shook her once. "I'll always find you. I'll always hunt you. It became a passion of mine while I sat in solitary confinement." His black-black eyes bored into hers and his fingers left marks on her arms.

Katie glanced down and saw one pistol in his double holster. She thought to grab it but Anthony shook her again until her head dropped back onto her shoulders. "Fight me, Katie. It'll make it much more pleasurable for me. I enjoy playing rough." He talked his way into her soul. He was the point man as Murphy described. He did not have to pull a trigger; he could simply scare her to death with his words. However, his disadvantage was that he did not believe Katie would fight him.

She spit in his face and when Ricci recoiled, Katie punched him hard on his wounded thigh.

Jake Cherry stood by the water and when he saw the struggle, he started to laugh until Katie turned toward him with Ricci's pistol in her hands. She pulled the trigger, but the shot went wild when Ricci kicked the back of her legs.

She landed hard but held on to the pistol. When Ricci

reached for her, she pulled the trigger again, and again, but the cartridge was empty.

He half-grimaced, half-smiled at her. "I only keep one bullet loaded, Katie. I only need one." He lay on his back as she did and he reached for her.

Katie threw the gun at his face.

She scrambled to her feet and ran before Ricci twisted around again. "Get her!" he screamed to Jake. "Get her now."

A small distance behind Ricci, the posse tracked the threesome. Murphy held the lantern low in order to see the ground. It was painful to bend forward and his head pounded a rhythm with each horse's step.

"Here," Todd said, coming along beside him with a packet of powder and a canteen. "It'll ease the pain."

"I can't take morphine," Murphy told him. "It'll dull my senses."

"It's not morphine. I put together a mixture that won't confuse your brain."

Spilling the powder into his mouth, he drank from the canteen and then handed it back to Todd. "She doesn't want to be with him, you realize that?"

"I don't know anything. She never told me what happened." He put the canteen back on his saddle. "She told me that she didn't want me to get hurt, that she thought I would go storming back to Chicago on the first stage."

"She was right," Murphy told him. "If she told you what she told me yesterday about the way Ricci treated her, you would've stormed back there, but it wouldn't have been your feelings that got hurt. Ricci would've cut you down where you stood."

"You know I may only be an egghead doctor but I can defend myself and my sister."

"I know you can, but Ricci got past me and he got past Buck. What do you think he would do to you?"

"But I love my sister. I would fight more arduously."

"Yes, and you would arduously die. And don't think that I won't protect her, Todd. I care about what happens to her."

"Do you?"

Murphy moved the lantern downward again and did not answer him.

Katie's feet slipped in the fallen leaves that were already damp with the night's mist. She fell on her side behind a log and then peeked out above it to see Jake Cherry. The moon silhouetted his body at the edge of the tree line.

Panic gripped her and Katie nearly got to her feet to run again. Instead, she lay still knowing Jake would catch her easily if she showed herself. If he got beyond the log then she would slip off in the opposite direction.

His boots crunched in the leaves and he breathed heavily. He neared the log and Katie saw that he had drawn his pistol. "Come on out, Katie," Jake called in a soft singsong voice. "Ricci wants to see you. He has all sorts of plans for you, sister. He shared some of them with me. I can tell you all about it if you like."

Katie trembled all over. Surely Jake heard her shaking in the leaves.

His voice grew confident, louder, as if he knew she was nearby. "If we have to hunt you down again, things will go badly for you." He stepped closer, holstered his gun, and started to laugh.

Blinding fear pushed Katie to her feet.

Jake caught her by the waist, spun her around, and then half-carried, half-pushed her out of the trees and back toward the horses.

Ricci was on his feet again. When she was close enough, he grabbed her arm and slapped her face. He held onto her tightly so that she would not fall and then he slapped her again.

Katie tasted blood in her mouth. She fought him like a wildcat until he grabbed her by the throat. Not able to breath, she clawed at his fingers.

He bent toward her. "If you run again I will kill you." Releasing her throat, he pushed her toward the horses. When she stumbled, he wound his hands in her hair and lifted her. "Get on the horse."

Murphy lay on his back staring straight through the pines and at the stars. After he had slumped in his saddle Buck grabbed him and helped him lie down. Todd thought that Murphy had a bad reaction to the headache powder and he covered Murphy with a blanket when the shakes started.

He woke near dawn when a long scream filled the forest. Buck and Todd saddled up. They believed it was Katie screaming. Murphy could have told them it was a mountain cat but they had not heard his objections.

Todd explained he would return for Murphy and instructed him to lie still. Murphy could not have moved even if the mountain cat came out of the trees to eat him.

Near noon he sat up with a mouth so dry he could spit dust. He tried whistling for his mount, and when that didn't work, he clicked his dry tongue. Indigo moved toward him and Murphy used the reins to pull himself upward. He found his canteen and after a while he mounted the horse.

Ricci's trail moved southwest and then climbed through steep woods. Finally, Murphy broke onto an open and rocky ridge. Below he saw a small lake and at the far end of it was a grove of oaks and pines. Tucked into the trees there stood a log cabin.

Murphy slouched in the saddle again. Things were catching up to him. He had been beaten, shot, left for dead, and now poisoned by his best friend. No wonder he went down so fast when someone hit him on the back of the head.

Ricci crouched in front of Murphy. "It seems many a dumb and useless human being can survive a shot to the chest."

Hands and feet bound, Murphy leaned against a log wall. He moved his head slightly to examine his surroundings and realized he sat on a dirt floor in the cabin by the lake. Katie Thomas sat next to the hearth. She looked unharmed, but then he saw the welt on her cheek and the bruise beneath it. A long scratch streaked her left arm and there were finger marks on her throat.

Ricci pulled a pistol and pointed it at Murphy's face. The barrel of it hit the bridge of his nose. "I wonder if you can survive a shot to the head."

"Anthony, no! . . ." Katie cried out and landed on her knees next to Ricci. She pushed his arm. "Don't kill him."

He smiled at her in a leering manner. "Why not, pretty Katie? Is he your lover?"

"Let me kill him, Anthony."

Ricci's brow raised a fraction. "You want to kill him?"

"Yes," she acted out. This would need to be her finest performance. "He . . . I hate him. He is the most arrogant man I've ever known. He accused me of thievery and murder and threatened to watch me hang until dead." She glanced at Murphy but not into his eyes. "Every day he taunted me and counted the hours until the circuit judge came to town. He served me rotten food just to torture me. I want to see him scared and I want to look into his eyes when he dies."

Ricci pulled the gun from Murphy face.

She said again, "Let me shoot him."

He holstered the weapon and dragged Katie to her feet. "I'm not going to give you a gun because I'm not stupid. I'll shoot him for you."

She softened her features and looked Ricci square on. She let her eyes travel his features, the same way he did to her in the parlor that day in her aunt's home. She kept her eyes on his mouth. In a quiet voice she said, "I know you're not stupid, Anthony. You're a clever man." She stepped closer.

He leaned back and she saw that his face was pale and sweaty. His leg still bled, by the look of it. Katie doubted he would assault her today or tonight. "What are you doing, Katie? You don't love me."

She gave him a coy smile. "Love? What is love, Anthony? That's not what I'm looking for. I only want to be with you for a little while. You're a man who knows about the world." She touched his shirt with both hands.

He grabbed her wrists. "Since when? You didn't want anything to do with me."

She shrugged. "It was just a game to pique your interest. That was why I followed you. I wanted—"

"Is that why you had Leonard arrest me?"

She tutted softly at him and pulled away. "I knew you'd get away. I'm surprised it took you so long. I had to get away from Chicago, Anthony. I had to get away from that horrid little girl's college and from Aunt Victoria and Nadine. I want to start over and I know you're the man to help me."

Ricci's eyes danced in the firelight. She had him interested. Would he give her the pistol?

"I'll tell you what I'll do. You may kill the sheriff in any way that you wish to, but not with a gun."

She thought quickly. "I want him to hang," Katie answered viciously, turning toward Murphy again but not meeting his eyes. "But I want to do it tomorrow so that he has all day and tonight to think about it. And then I want to watch him swing."

"Why, Katie," Anthony cooed, "I think I love you."

She put on her best smile and finally gazed at Murphy.

He stared back at her with a look she had seen many times before. It was one of complete suspicion and distrust.

Ricci stepped in front of Katie and announced to Murphy, "It's a great gift I'm going to give to you today, Sheriff: the wrath of a truly magnificent woman." Then he moved toward the table to pull a whiskey bottle out of his satchel. He had taken three from Buck's storeroom. "Never mind a glass," he told Katie. "I'll take mine whole." His eyes darted past hers to study the cabin. They stood in its only room and it was squalid and filthy, with assorted rubbish on the floor. A corn-silk mattress lay in the corner. The table had three chairs with two cups and a dish on top. A black pot hung on a pole over the fire and there was one window facing the lake.

Ricci twisted the top off the bottle. "Did I ever tell you about my family, Katie? We lived in a sty like this. My mother didn't like housework; she liked this stuff." He held up the bottle. "And she liked to slap us around and box our ears. When I was little she used to trip me and laugh about it, may she rot in hell." He took a long drink and pulled a chair to sit it by the window. "Well, would you listen to me? I'm feeling quite homesick." He sat in the chair and faced the window. "I hate looking at filth. It disturbs me. Would you tidy up while I rest, Katie?"

Jake Cherry returned to the cabin with a squirrel and a rabbit. "Why is he still alive?" He tossed the dead animals onto the table and glared at Murphy. Pulling his pistol, he took aim.

Ricci did not turn around. "He's alive because Katie wished it."

Jake eyed her now. With heavy sarcasm, he replied, "Well, if Katie wants it that way." He holstered his pistol and glanced at Ricci. "Does that also mean he gets a draw of the money?"

"We'll talk about it later," Ricci answered.

"We'll talk about it now."

Katie backed away when Ricci slowly rose from his chair. "Are you questioning me?"

Jake took his hand off his weapon and let it drop to his side.

"You, who I sent to do a simple task. . . . *Get Katie and the money,* I said. *Bring her to me.* Did you? No, I had to saddle up and ride in myself."

Jake pointed at Murphy. "He shot me." He pulled his weapon again and squeezed the trigger. The bullet went through a log right above Murphy's head.

Katie had covered her mouth and stared at Murphy but quickly dropped her hands to her side. She did not want Anthony to see her fear for Murphy's life.

Ricci did not look at her. With the whiskey bottle still in his hand, he smashed it hard against the table. Glass shattered and the whiskey sprayed upward. Now he held the neck of it like a knife and pointed it at Jake. He slashed at him.

Jake backed away.

"*I* say *when* he dies."

Jake raised his hands. "All right, all right . . ."

"If I decide to give him all the money, you will like it, and you will thank me for doing it."

"All right, sure."

"KATIE."

Her heart lurched.

"Come here, Katie," Ricci said, calming at last. He looked at her and pointed to the glass. "Clean this quickly. I don't like it. It upsets me. Jake, take these animals outside to skin." He limped to the table and removed a new bottle from the saddlebags. Then he returned to his chair.

Katie found a cloth and brushed the glass pieces into her hand. She threw them into the fireplace. Whatever alcohol touched the flames sparked and the fire danced. With her boot, she kicked an especially large piece toward the grate, but then hesitated. She turned to see Jake walk out the door, and then she bent to pick up the glass to tuck into her pocket.

With the little supplies she had, she cooked meat stew. A while later, she ladled portions for each person into the cups and plate she'd found. She handed the largest to Ricci. He smiled at her and brought one hand to her waist. It did not appear that the whiskey affected him except that he seemed to be in less pain. He said, "Sit with me for a moment?" His voice was a silken grumble.

Katie leaned on the windowsill. She heard the call of a jay.

"I've decided not to return to Springfield. I think it would be wiser to go on to California . . . with you. That way you can be away from your family and we can be together. There are all sorts of opportunities there for an enterprising couple."

Katie realized she should smile at the news. "I think we'll be happy there."

"We'll need money, of course, but now that my leg is injured I won't be able to throw over another stage for a while." He twisted in his seat, grimacing, "We'll have to use your money to get there."

"My money?" she asked, watching Jake stand and walk toward the table. He acted interested in their conversation.

"Yes, your money. The money you took from the stage."

"I didn't take money from the stage."

His hand reached for her wrist and he held it tightly. "Of course you did."

She tried to pull her hand away and pushed off the windowsill. "What do you know about it?"

He held her wrist tightly. "We were there, Jake and I."

"You robbed the stage?"

Ricci laughed at her. "No, I didn't. I shot a bunch of people and as entertaining as that was, I didn't get any cash for my trouble."

Her chest tightened. "Why does everyone think I stole the money?"

Jake Cherry walked toward her. "I don't know why everyone else does but I saw you do it."

"You saw me?"

"That's right. I rode over the hill just as you pulled the moneybag from the driver's locker. Hank climbed out of the cab just as you ran off."

"Why would I take the money?"

Ricci stroked her wrist. "It's all right, Katie. Did you think I'd be angry? I'm not. I'm pleasantly surprised." He pulled her toward his chair. "Regardless, we need the cash. Where is it?"

"I don't now where the money is."

He pulled her downward until her cheek touched his. "Did you give it to Hank?"

She pulled away to stare into his black eyes. "I don't know anyone named Hank."

Ricci laughed at that. He let her stand but kept hold of her wrist. "Hank Walker, a man I'd call my equal. You turned him in at the same time you turned me in, sweetheart. Was it only me that you had eyes for?" His fingers tightened. "He boarded the stage with you in Lincoln. He told me at the wreckage site that you recognized him and that you only paid attention to the young man. That's why I shot the young man, Katie. I shot him because you liked him. It's your fault, you know? I sent Hank after you. Did you give him the money?"

"Hank Walker is dead." Murphy spoke from the corner by the hearth. "She killed him. I found him in the woods when I searched for her."

Everyone stared at Katie and then Ricci laughed in delight. "Did you? Good for you, Katie, and, not that I care, but why did you do it? Did he try to take the money from you?" When he saw the look of horror on her face, he said. "It doesn't matter. Tomorrow you will take me to the money and we will be on our way."

* * *

Katie stared into the fire for a long time. She had another headache but she did not dare lie down to sleep. Morning would come and Jake would hang Murphy. She had to do something.

She ladled meat stew into the cup and then she moved to kneel in front of the sheriff. She met his cold gray-blue eyes. Did he hate her again? She put the spoon to his lips but he did not open his mouth.

Katie pivoted her body sideways to view Ricci. When she did it, she removed the glass shard from her pocket and slipped it into Murphy's bound hand so that he might cut his way through the roping. She turned to look at him again. His eyes were no longer cold, only questioning. She returned to the fire to stir the meat stew.

The sun went down. The only light came from the fire in the hearth. Ricci had fallen asleep by the window. He had drunk at least three-quarters of a bottle of straight whiskey. Jake, however, had not touched the liquor and he appeared alert at his post by the door. He pulled his pistol from the holster to rub a cloth over the barrel of it. Katie wondered where Jake and Ricci had met: Springfield, Chicago, or prison. Jake Cherry probably figured he had hitched his wagon to a star.

Katie sat at the table pretending to sleep but watching Jake. She had to get past him. Turning toward Murphy, she saw that he concentrated on his task. His arms barely moved. Suddenly, his shoulders jerked. Had he cut through the rope? He stared hard at Katie.

She sat up and pretended to rub sleep from her eyes.

Murphy nodded toward his boots. He needed to untie them but Jake watched him every second or so.

Katie would have to create a diversion. But how? She gazed at Ricci, still sleeping, and then she smiled at Jake. He did not look at her just then, so she stood and walked toward him.

He glanced at her and then narrowed his watery eyes.

Katie moved closer, bent toward him, and whispered, "Would you take me for a walk?"

Jake threw the cloth aside. His heavy whiskered face lifted in suspicion. At this proximity, Katie saw the pock-marks on one side of his nose. "What are you up to, sister?"

"Well . . . the thing is . . ." She stepped closer, tore the shoulder seam of her blouse, and let out a high-pitched scream.

Jake's eyes bulged and he stood quickly to slap his hand over her mouth.

Ricci vaulted from the chair to take in the scene.

"It was her!" Jake squealed, releasing Katie so that she fell against the wall. He pointed at her. "She came at me, she wanted me . . ."

Ricci charged him. Jake tried to get the door opened but Ricci sprang at him. They both fell onto the chair and it broke into pieces.

Katie danced away from their kicking feet and rushed to Murphy's side. He cut quickly through the rope and then jumped to his feet. "Come on," he growled, pulling her across the room. Suddenly Murphy lifted Katie from behind and then shoved her out the opened window. Before she rolled to her knees, the sheriff landed next to her. "Move," he commanded and pushed her toward the trees.

Walls of darkness towered on every side as the trees enveloped them. Murphy grabbed Katie's elbow and pulled her toward the left. He ducked past low branches and crashed through waist-high bushes, dragging her along behind him. "Where are we going?" she asked, breathless, trying to keep up with him.

Murphy slowed and stared at the lake. "Well," he replied, catching his breath, "we're going to . . . somehow we need to get my horse and my rifle."

"Where are they?"

"At the cabin."

"Terrific."

"Yup."

They hurried along again, picking their way over logs and through brush. They weaved in and out another minute and then dove for cover when a gunshot exploded behind them.

Katie lay on her belly in the dirt with Murphy at her side. She glanced behind them. Nothing moved. "Where did it come from?"

Murphy nodded toward the left. "From the cabin."

"Ricci must've shot him."

"I'd be happier if Jake shot Ricci." He crawled forward to watch the area near the cabin.

Katie crawled after him.

Suddenly Murphy turned on her. "You know you were a bit reckless in the way you spoke to him." He said it in a low tone but she heard his ill humor.

"Reckless?"

Murphy pointed toward the cabin. "He's crazy."

"I *know* that!" It was hard to argue while keeping her voice so low.

He leaned toward her. "Well, if you knew that why did you tempt him? He could have killed us both."

"Why did I tempt him?" she asked incredulously.

Murphy turned away from her.

She tapped him on the shoulder. When he frowned at her, she informed him, "If I remember rightly, *and I do,* I saved your life."

"No, you took twenty years off my life."

"Well, the least you can do is thank me."

When he said nothing, she pushed to her knees.

Her movement caused him to jerk toward her. "Hey! Hey, hey . . ." He grabbed her boot. "Get down here."

Something moved at them from their right side and Katie hit the dirt next to Murphy again.

He pushed her head down and looked overtop her. "Stay still," Murphy whispered, and then, "Something's following our scent. Can you climb a tree?"

Katie nodded.

"It might be a wolf . . ." Twenty seconds went by. "I am going to let go of you. Climb a tree as quickly as you can. I will be right behind you."

Fear paralyzed Katie. She did not want to move from her spot.

"Now," Murphy barked.

She did not move fast enough and Murphy snatched her by the arm. Katie sailed a foot before hitting the ground to run.

Murphy jumped at a low limb and swung his leg over the branch. He held his hand out for her to grab.

A large amorphous shape charged the tree.

It wasn't a wolf! Hopping and screeching, Katie grabbed at Murphy's hand.

A three-hundred-pound bear wrapped its paw around Katie's middle and snatched her out of the air. Big Buck said, "I'm glad to see you again, Katie Thomas."

In reply, she fainted in his arms.

A moment later, Katie woke in Todd's arms. He cradled her there on the forest floor and pushed her hair out of her face. "Everything is fine," he cooed. "I'm here." When her eyes fluttered opened, Todd let her head fall into the leaves and dirt. "You've got a lot of explaining to do, Katie! What do you mean by running off with Anthony Ricci?"

Katie rubbed her sore head while frowning at her brother.

Murphy let out a laugh and she scowled at him too. He held a pistol in his hand again and looked much more daring with it. "I'm going after Ricci," he told Buck and Todd. "First I need to return to the cabin and find Indigo."

"There's a cabin out here?" Buck asked.

Murphy studied him in the half light. "What have you been tracking all day?"

"Well, we followed a wildcat for a while."

"Then Buck stumbled upon a black bear," Todd added. "That was memorable."

Buck nodded. "For the last couple of hours we'd lost our way and tried to figure out which side of the tree the moss is growing on."

"Then we heard a gunshot," Todd explained.

"That's when I saw Katie jumping up and down trying to get into this tree."

Murphy nodded and raised a brow at Katie. Turning to Buck again, he asked, "Where are your horses?"

"Right over here," Buck told him, leading the way.

Todd asked Murphy, "Should I take Katie back to town?"

"No," he replied, shrugging out of the way of a low branch. "I don't know where Ricci is right now. He could track you."

Todd stopped and turned around in the dirt. "What does he want, Katie? I thought this was all over. Now he shows up to what, break you out of jail?"

Katie would have explained but Murphy spoke over her, "They hatched up a plot together to hang me tomorrow, and after that they are going to run away to California together."

The man was impossible. He did not appreciate a thing!

Chapter Seven

"**I** know I left Naggy right here," Buck said, spinning in the clearing. He peered behind the nearest tree as though his horse hid from him.

Katie sat on a boulder with her knees up and her elbows propped. She thought she might as well get comfortable as she suspected it would be a long night. But her mood was light. They had escaped Ricci, and the sheriff, although irritating and mocking as ever, did not act as though he thought she was a criminal anymore.

Todd stood in the middle of the clearing scratching his jaw. "We didn't leave the horses here. There was a river nearby and I saw a bridge."

Murphy leaned on the boulder Katie sat on. She told him, "I see you picked your finest trackers."

He shrugged and then looked into her eyes. "I wanted to be the one to save you."

What was this? Was he flirting with her? Murphy, *the*

Murphy who coldly accused her of killing and thieving two weeks ago? "Don't start that again," she told him, refusing to look at him.

"Start what?"

"Testing me to see how fast I fall for sweet talk and manipulation."

He shook his head, keeping his eyes fixed on her. "I'm only testing to see how quickly you fall for me."

He could not be serious, although Katie had to admit that he looked serious. His eyes held hers for a long moment as his hand reached out to touch a lock of her hair. He leaned toward her as his eyes riveted to her lips.

Katie pushed off the rock and backed away. "I told you. I knew it!"

"Knew what?"

"Barlett Sanders."

"Barlett . . . ?"

She backed away. "I won't have anything to do with you now."

The truth was it would take so little for her to have something to do with Wade Murphy. It was as though seeds of affection had been planted in her heart the past few weeks and all it would take was a small amount of attention from the sheriff, and those seeds would blossom into full-grown love.

Even in the moonlight, she saw Murphy's gray eyes brighten. "I'm no Barlett Sanders, count on that. Do you really believe that I can be brushed off so easily?" He took a step around the boulder. "Have I not proven that I'm a determined man, Miss Thomas, and that I'll stop at nothing to get what I want?"

Katie's heart hammered. My goodness but she fell fast. She took another step away from him. "You've only proven that you make assumptions and can nearly get yourself killed by Anthony Ricci."

Murphy shook his head and took another step.

"And then I had to come up with a plan to rescue you."

Murphy caught her hand and pulled it to his chest. "I guess the least I can do is thank you."

Breathless now, she told him. "Yes, that's the least . . ."

"What is the *most* I can do to thank you?"

Todd called to them, "I know where the horses are! Follow me."

Murphy held Katie's hand as they walked. What the man did to her senses! She was as dizzy as she was clear-headed. He did not look at her again but helped her over logs and pushed brush from her path.

Ten minutes later Katie heard the sound of water. They walked near a ridge with a moderately steep drop-off. Beneath it, the Platte River ran swift and deep. "I don't see a bridge," Buck complained, "or my horse."

Murphy took the lead. "There's a bridge farther up-river."

Five minutes later, Katie saw the outline of a rotted timber bridge with no handrails and with several planks missing. Buck approached the ridge and gazed over the side of it.

"No horses down there," Todd told him, looking around the clearing. "But they've got to be close by." He walked toward Katie and Murphy. "The man can pour a fine drink but he can't walk a straight path."

"Watch out," Katie squealed when something dark and alive sprang out of the bushes right next to Buck.

Jake Cherry rushed him. The bartender might not have been his first choice to assault but Buck stood closest to the bush. Jake stuck a pistol into his side.

Todd and Murphy both snapped their pistols off their belts and took aim at Jake while blocking Katie from him.

"Gentlemen," Jake greeted, staying behind Buck and using him as a shield. "Sheriff, I'll make a deal with you. I'll trade you this here fella for Katie Thomas."

"No deal," Buck answered for Murphy.

Jake spat on the ground. "Shut up. I'm not talking to you. What about it, Sheriff? I'll switch you and I won't kill the girl if we do this polite-like. If there's no deal then I'll kill all of you."

"You're no killer," Murphy told him, stepping forward. "But I'll make a deal with you. Put down the weapon and lead me to Ricci. I'll make sure you get a fair trial and a bargain for turning him over to me."

Jake laughed while he tried to keep an eye on Buck and the two men in front of him. "Two things, Sheriff, two things you ought to know about me. One is that I ain't no snitch."

"That's very Christian of you," Buck told him.

"And number two, I *am* a killer. I just shot Anthony Ricci, I did. I shot him right in the chest. He bled all over the place."

Murphy took slow steps to the right.

Todd took two slow steps to the left and said conversationally, "What do you want with my sister?"

Katie stayed in step behind Todd.

Their strategy worked. Jake acted nervous, swinging his eyes between the two men. "What I want is the money and Katie is going to take me to it."

"Don't you know that she doesn't remember anything about that day? She doesn't know where the money is."

Jake spat on the ground again. "She remembers."

"No she doesn't," Todd continued, taking another slow step. "In the medical profession we call the condition amnesia."

"Well in the outlaw profession we call it lying. Now both of you stop moving or I'll gun this man down."

Murphy had Jake in his sights and he lifted the pistol eye level.

Jake took his weapon from Buck's side and raised it toward the sheriff.

For such a large man, Buck moved gracefully as he pirouetted around and jabbed the back of his elbow into Jake's nose.

Jake flew spread-eagle and landed on his shoulders.

Buck was on him, grabbed him by the shirt and belt, and then lifted the man high overtop his head.

Jake hollered so loudly that night birds flew off their branches and the squirrels ran for cover.

"Put him down," Murphy called to Buck. "I'll take it from here," he told him, but Katie was not sure that Buck heard him, what with Jake hollering the way he did. Jake kept screaming right up to the time that Buck threw him over the ledge.

"Oh my," Katie said in a rush as she joined Todd, Buck, and Murphy on the ridge's brink. There came the sound of a splash thirty or forty feet beneath them and then in the moonlight Katie saw Jake Cherry surface with his arms flailing and his feet kicking. The current swept him up and sent him traveling fast downstream.

"You might've killed him," Todd said in amazement.

"He's too dirty and smelly to die. Besides, that's what he gets for stealing three bottles of whiskey from my storeroom."

"You're a dangerous man to tangle with," Murphy said, slapping him on the back.

Buck nodded. "I feel so good. There ain't nothing like a gun in the gut for a man to take stock of his life." He walked toward the clearing with the rest of them. "I believe I will turn over a new leaf."

Todd stared at him. "You mean you're going to stop cussing and drinking and raising the devil in that business you call a saloon?"

Buck stared at him. "No, I'm talking about being a kinder and gentler . . . you think I drink too much?"

"I think you do everything too much."

Katie interrupted the argument by spotting movement in the clearing. "Is that your horse?"

"Naggy," he cried joyfully.

Smoke still curled from the chimney but all else was quiet when they approached the cabin. Murphy and Todd rode double and Murphy dismounted first to crouch low when he reached the window. He lifted himself enough to peek inside the shack and then he stood.

Buck held out his arm for Katie to dismount and he came off the horse to stand next to her. By then Murphy had moved to the back of the cabin with his pistol drawn. When he returned, he led his stallion by the reins and carried his rifle over his shoulder.

"Shouldn't there be a dead man in here?" Todd asked when he stepped through the door.

Katie picked her way past the broken chair and went to stoke the fire.

"There's blood on the floor," Murphy pointed out. "But it might be from his leg wound." He kicked the remains of the chair into a corner.

"Wait a minute," Buck asked through the window. "Are you saying Jake Cherry lied to us?"

Todd knelt beside the droplets. "This isn't enough to suggest a fatal wound. Jake didn't kill Anthony Ricci."

Katie kept her back to the men. Ricci was not dead. That meant he would come for her again.

Buck came into the cabin and stared at the floor. "I've dropped more blood from a cut finger. The man is only hurt enough to make him mad. He'll come back hell-bent."

Katie's sigh caused the three to stare her direction.

"Sorry," Buck mumbled. "That was insensitive of me."

Katie shook her head. "It's all right, Buck."

Murphy approached and then hunkered down in front of her. "Don't be frightened. We'll protect you."

"What makes you think I am frightened? I have the three finest men from Victor City protecting me."

Buck clapped Todd on the back. "That's right, ma'am. Ain't nobody gonna harm a hair on your head while we're watching over you. We'd all sacrifice our own lives for you." He grabbed Todd's shoulder and squeezed until the doctor grimaced. "Starting with Todd here."

Murphy got to his feet. "Buck, take watch at the window. I'll guard the door." He grabbed a chair from the table in the center of the room.

Todd asked, "What's the plan now?"

"We wait until daylight," Murphy answered and shoved the chair against the door, sat and leaned back in it.

Katie's head found the wall and she watched Murphy through her lashes.

Buck asked, "You think Ricci will return?"

Murphy answered while smiling at Katie. "If he does, I'll arrest him tonight instead of tomorrow." He laid his rifle across his lap and with his finger on the trigger.

A storm raged. Lightning hit the ground and caught fire in the woods. The fire made a circle around Katie. Then, in lightning form again, it struck left, right, and hit behind her. The thunder sounded as though it spoke "Katie Thomas!"

She started to run but lightning struck the earth in front of her. Hands of fire grabbed her shoulders and threw her to the ground. Dazzling light came at her until the thunder spoke again and the lightning died and blood covered the front of her.

Katie came full awake with a scream on her lips. She choked it back before it escaped. A drop of sweat rolled down the side of her face and the front of her blouse stuck to her ribcage. She saw Buck still sitting at the window but Todd had fallen asleep at the table. His blond head rested on his arms.

Murphy stared at her. He frowned when he saw the look in her eyes and he started to rise from the chair. She held up a hand to stop him and whispered, "It was just a dream. I am all right."

Still frowning, he took his seat again.

Katie wiped perspiration from her hairline and noticed Buck staring at her too. She did not realize how her face had paled or how her lips trembled. When Buck looked at Murphy with raised brows, Katie closed her eyes again. She woke the next morning to see Murphy standing at the table with Buck and Todd. A pot of beans warmed on the fire, compliments of Buck's stocked saddlebags. Her stomach growled. It was not pancakes and bacon but the beans tasted wonderful. Katie ate while listening to the men's conversation.

"Ricci headed north," Murphy told the others. "I found tracks when the sun came up."

Todd added, "If he's heading north then that means he's headed for Victor City."

Murphy eyed Katie. "I believe he is."

Katie knew Ricci would still come for her. He had said he would.

Buck asked, "He's still looking for the money?" He sat next to Katie with his huge belly hanging over his belt. His muscular forearms seemed as big as her waist.

Murphy pushed at the plate in front of him. He stood and grabbed his rifle. "As soon as everyone is ready we need to head out." He went to the door and stood outside.

Katie collected the tins and stacked them neatly after scraping them. When she handed them to Buck, he stuffed them into his saddlebag.

She rode with Todd, sitting behind him in the saddle. They headed north and then east over the rocky ridge. Murphy led the way. Hours later, the sun turned hot. Katie wished she could bathe. It had been two days since her last bath and it was not as if she had been sitting idle in the parlor. She glanced down at her white blouse that was now brown stained and ripped at the shoulder. Dirt smeared her pants. Her hair curled and knotted and she knew there were little bits of twigs and leaves in it.

Murphy called a halt next to a stream. Katie washed her face and hands while Buck rummaged through saddlebags for more food. Murphy stood next to Katie. He watched her with his rifle on one shoulder. Katie squinted up at him because the sun was straight behind him. Looking somber, he set the rifle beside him and splashed water onto his face and arms. "Have you always had nightmares, Katie?"

"Not that I remember."

"You were terrified when you woke last night."

She scrubbed her nails. "It was a bad dream."

"Do you remember any of it?"

She studied him. His dark hair waved on either side of his face and there was two days' worth of growth on his chin. "Lightning, I think."

"You had bad dreams while you were in jail. I heard you at night sometimes."

She shrugged and rubbed her hands.

He stood with his rifle on his shoulder again and gazed at the sky. A mass of thunderheads loomed over a distant range of mountains.

Katie stood too. "Murphy?"

"Hmm?"

"Do I have to go to jail when we return to Victor City?"

The question seemed to surprise him, as if he had not thought about it. "No. There will have to be some sort of presentation to the circuit judge though. Money is still missing and there were five deaths, maybe six if Ben doesn't pull through. There are a lot of questions left unanswered."

"Like what?"

"Everyone, including Ben Raines, said you took the money."

Katie remembered. She had been beneath the bed when Ben told the sheriff that she took the moneybag. She also remembered how she had slid out the window and down the balcony post. She accused, "You tried to shoot me."

"Pardon?"

"When you came out onto the balcony from Ben's window, you took a shot at me."

He gave her a quick grin. "If I'd meant to shoot you, Katie, I would have." He studied the sky again. "But your stubborn hide wouldn't take a warning and you kept running."

"I'm not stubborn."

"Oh no, not much, you ain't."

Katie smiled at that. "I tried to regain my memory but you didn't act as though you wanted to help me."

"You're right, Katie." He said earnestly and his gray-blue eyes held hers. "I was arrogant and I thought I knew everything. In my mind, you were guilty because my gut told me you were guilty. I'd never been wrong about behavior before, but I was this time, and I'm sorry."

"It's all right," she whispered, suddenly shy.

He smiled at her. "You're sweet and I will believe everything you tell me from now on."

She smiled too but his words made her think of something. "Why did you tell Ricci that I killed Hank Walker?"

"There was no one else out there, Katie, and you carried the gun that the bullet matched."

Katie wished she felt as confident about matters as Murphy did. But he was wrong about this. He must be! "There has to be another explanation," she told him, now cross. "You said Sheriff Bates was in the woods too. He might've killed—"

"Ricci killed Bates. The bullets match. I already figured it out."

"Just like you figured out that I robbed the stage, is that what you mean?" She had not meant to sound so spiteful, but she was not a killer. Did Murphy still suspect her? Had he only been nice to her because he felt guilty over the way he treated her? Obviously Murphy believed she took the money.

Exasperation flashed in Murphy's eyes. "Bullet-matching isn't my opinion, it's a science. The same bullet that killed Bates killed Foster Garrett. Anthony Ricci admitted to both murders. The bullet that killed Darryl came from Jake Cherry's rifle. The thing I was wrong about was that whoever shot Darryl was a sharp-shooter. Jake Cherry got lucky with his shot. The gun you carried killed Hank Walker. It also shot Ben Raines, the professor, and the actor, Theodore Moon."

"What professor?"

"Professor James Caldwell."

Katie's mind flashed to the face of an elderly gentleman. He had dark gray hair and a white beard. "You're causing the woman distress," he had said. "Stop staring at her," and then he had fallen sideways when a bullet caught him in the heart.

"So you somehow took the gun from Hank Walker."

Katie knit her brow. "What are you talking about?" Her head hurt so badly all of a sudden. The sun felt like a knife in her eyes.

"That has to be it, Katie. Hank shot the professor, Moon, and Ben. You took the gun from him."

"How could I do that? The man was almost the size of Big Buck."

"You remember him?"

"Remember who?"

Frustrated, Murphy watched her. "Hank Walker. You just said he was almost the size of Big Buck."

"Can we talk about this later? My head hurts." Perhaps Todd had something in his saddlebags.

"Why did you aim to shoot me that day? Why did you want to kill me?"

Light, bright, flashing . . . "Because you called my name."

"What?"

Katie stared at Murphy again. "What?"

"You said you meant to shoot me because I called you by name."

She laughed at him. For the life of her, Katie did not know what he talked about now. "You don't make any sense, Murphy."

"A storm is coming," Buck called to them as he led his horse to the stream. He carried beef jerky in his hand and gave a chunk to Katie.

Murphy did not move away from the stream when Katie did. She did not know that he stared after her for a long time.

Buck had left Naggy by the stream and walked with Katie toward Todd. He stopped midstride and watched the doctor.

Todd stretched his arms over his head and then kicked his feet in the air. Taking a deep breath, he rolled his shoulders.

"He's exercising," Katie explained, recognizing her brother's routine.

"I wondered if it was some sort of dance or if he's chasing evil spirits from these mountains."

Todd ran in place. "You don't have a clue about what I'm doing, big fella." He pushed his spectacles back onto his nose.

"Yes, I do. You're irritating me."

"You need to start an exercise program or your heart is going to give out on you." He jogged around Buck in a circle. "There is a lot of evidence, medically speaking, that points to early death in obese bartenders."

"Obese? How about I start my exercise program by breaking your little twig body over my knee?"

Todd ran in place in front of him. He did not look the least threatened. "You might start by not drinking so much and pushing yourself away from the table."

Buck's face turned red. "You know, for a doctor, you don't know so much about staying healthy."

Katie turned to watch Murphy. He walked by the stream. Then he crossed the shallow water and studied the opposite shore. At last, he crossed again and grabbed his horse's reins. "He crossed the stream."

Katie asked, "Is that bad?"

Todd looked where Murphy gazed into the recesses of the forest beyond the stream. "It means he didn't go to Victor City."

Murphy said, "He knows I am coming for him. He's waiting for me."

"You think he is setting a trap?" Buck asked, mounting his own stallion.

"Maybe." Murphy watched the hills and boulders. The rim of his hat darkened his face so that Katie could not read his expression.

Ready to mount, Todd asked, "Should I take Katie back to town now?"

Murphy turned to look at them. "Yes. It will take you the rest of the afternoon but you should be able to make it to town before the storm blows in." His eyes went to the thunderheads moving slowly in their direction. "Get to the Overland and stay on it. If we're not back in town by morning, form a new posse."

His words scared Katie. What if morning came and Murphy didn't? She would never get over it if that were to happen. Murphy asked her, "Would you like to take my rifle? Buck has a six-shooter that I can use and Todd has a pistol."

Katie shook her head and shielded her eyes from the sun. "I'm not worrying over me," she told him.

He gave her a small smile and then raised his hand in the signal to move out.

Todd and Katie watched them cross the stream. When they disappeared into the trees, Todd boosted her into the saddle and then followed her up. "You like him, don't you?"

She did not answer him but smiled without turning around.

"Are you in love?" He leaned to the side to try to catch her eyes. "I knew it. I knew you two would hit it off."

"What if I do love him? That doesn't mean Murphy returns affection for me. He still thinks I am a criminal."

Todd scoffed at her. "I think it's obvious that you had nothing to do with the stage holdup, Katie. Murphy wouldn't let me take you to town if he thought you were guilty of a crime. He would keep you close by his side."

Funny, that was exactly where Katie wanted to be.

Buck followed Murphy through the deepening woods. The trees stood close together as the horses moved up the side of the mountain. Boulders appeared here and there and were much larger than the ones at the river-bank. The wind rustled the leaves in the trees.

Buck twisted around, raising his buffalo gun, and lowering it. "I can't tell the difference between the sound of the creaking branches and the sound of footsteps." He pulled the gun close to his belly and kept a close watch. "It makes me all-overish to think a character like Ricci is lying in wait for us ready to spring up like some twisted jack-in-the-box."

When they approached a stony ridge, Murphy held up his hand to stop. Dismounting, he studied the prints. Hoof marks slid to a stop near a boulder. One footprint marred the dirt. Murphy looked at Buck. "The tracks split two separate directions."

The statement startled Buck. "We're only tracking one man, ain't we?" He wiped his forehead and replaced his hat. "Old Gertie would call that black magic . . ."

"Footprints lead east toward the ridge," Murphy explained. "The horse tracks go southeast."

"Do you think he killed himself by leaping over the ridge?"

Murphy shrugged. "That would make things easy for us."

"I'd rather deal with the living, thank you. If he jumped we will have to do business with his ghost."

"What are you talking about?"

"I'm saying I would rather shoot it out with the bleeding sort than worry about Ricci's ghost haunting this hillside. Things are creepy enough up here without thinking about that."

"I'll follow the footprints," Murphy told him, dismounting. "Why don't you find out where the horse wandered off to? Give me a signal if you see anything."

Buck kneed his mount southeastward. "How about a high girlish scream?"

Murphy studied the two prints coming from the same boot. He glanced over the boulders and down the cliff.

Seeing no bloody remains, he backed up and turned to climb down again.

Ricci stood there looking wild with his hair standing straight on end. Blood covered the front of his vest from a shoulder wound; more blood stained his pant leg. He took a step and jumped toward Murphy to knock him backward.

Murphy's heart pumped hard as Ricci took the upper hand and pushed him toward the cliff's edge. He felt himself slipping on the dusty rocks and tried to get his hand on something solid.

Ricci fell backward, kicked Murphy's foot, and then screamed triumphantly when the sheriff lost his hand-hold.

Murphy fell eight feet before grabbing hold of a mis-routed tree root. His momentum tore open the wound on his chest. The pain of it seared through his side and arm. Ricci laughed above him and then a bullet whistled past the sheriff's good arm. Grabbing another hold on the rift, Murphy tried to flatten himself against the rock wall.

Another bullet barely missed his shoulder.

The sound of a buffalo rifle cracked overhead and Ricci moved away from the cliff edge. His bass voice drifted over the side, "Put the rifle in the scabbard and get off your horse."

Again the rifle sounded. Buck was far better at fighting a man with his bare hands than trying to shoot him. Murphy knew if the bartender got his hands on Ricci there would be no contest.

Murphy inched his way up the rock face. He heard

Buck shouting overhead and more gunfire splitting the air. He found crevices, one after the other, and pulled himself up by the fingertips. His chest burned like fire.

Ricci shouted, "Come on out, old man. You can't stay hidden behind a slab smaller than your backside."

Nearing the top of the ledge, Murphy sought a last handclasp. He moved left just as a knife fell over the rocks and into the canyon. He imagined Buck planned it for Ricci and missed.

He waited, listening. Horse hooves pounded toward the west and then Buck's voice called to him from overhead. "Give me your hand."

Relieved to see him alive, Murphy stuck his good arm into the air.

Buck lifted him easily. "Ricci is crazed," he said, pulling Murphy by the belt until he lay on his back on the boulders. "He looked like a half-starved wolf."

"He fooled me," Murphy admitted, rolling to his knees, and then standing. "He waited in the rocks." He took the lead down the slab to find his horse waiting by the trees. "Are you hurt?"

"Light on my feet as usual," Buck told him. "Naggy is heading west with Ricci, though. Hey, you're bleeding again."

"It's only a scratch." He mounted his stallion and held out his arm for the bartender to grab.

Buck shook his head. "I'll weigh you down."

"Do you have a weapon?"

"I have an empty gun, another skinning knife, and my bare hands. They'll do me fine."

Chapter Eight

T odd reined northward on the stage trail and urged the horse into a sensible gallop. Thunderclouds moved in on their left and Katie watched them for a moment, feeling drowsy with the rhythm of the ride—until she heard pounding hooves behind them. She twisted to look beyond Todd's shoulder, hoping to see Murphy and Buck.

It was Ricci.

A shotgun blast cracked the air.

Todd spurred Sawbones roughly and the usually placid gelding exploded into full gallop. Katie did not think they could outrun Ricci and she thought to defend them. A Hawken six-shooter lay tucked into a holster beneath the saddle. She tried pulling the pistol from the leather but it took plenty of maneuvering with the rhythm of horse's gait. When at last she snatched the weapon free, she swung her arm onto Todd's shoulder for support and took a shot.

Todd's eyes bulged and he hollered, "What are you doing?"

"Hold still," Katie shouted and took aim again. It was near impossible to get a clear shot with the pace they maintained. She took another try and missed, but it was close enough to make Ricci duck his head and lose ground. She saw that he rode Buck's horse and her stomach fell. Where was Buck? Where was Murphy?

Todd spurred Sawbones to the left. Spying a huge boulder, he pulled toward it. As they neared the rock, he grabbed Katie around the waist, and dove for cover.

"Give me the pistol," he shouted, pushing her body off his leg and struggling to his knees. He raised himself enough to glance out from the rock and took a shot at Ricci, who came up the slope after them.

The bullet missed and hit a tree instead.

Anthony slid from the horse and dove into the trees.

"Pull some ammunition from my belt," Todd instructed. "Why is it whenever I'm involved in one of your little adventures I wind up in a gunfight?"

Katie handed him the bullets and then ducked when one ricocheted off a nearby tree. "Two other times," she countered. "Two times is not every time."

Todd did not look at her. He shoved the bullets into the cartridge. His blond hair hung in his face as he worked. Brushing at it, he peered around the boulder.

Ricci glided through the tree line like a slippery snake to make himself a hard target.

"Why can't you stay home and make tapestries like other ladies?" Todd wanted to know, determined to stay angry with her. He took another shot and missed. "You were never content to learn womanly arts, were you? No, you wanted to rope and ride and shoot a gun."

"Todd, will you shut up and shoot the man?" She knew she said the words loudly but Katie was surprised to hear her voice vibrate off the western rock face and echo down the hill. Ricci's shots were riotous after that. One of the bullets pinged off the boulder in front of her and Katie fell to her belly.

White rocks lay scattered at the base of the boulder. Katie selected two of them and peeked around the big rock. She saw Ricci from her position. He looked dreadful with his shirt draped out of his pants on one side, his vest unbuttoned, and his black hair falling into his eyes. Blood stained his white shirt.

Katie brought her feet beneath her. Still crouching, she threw two of rocks, one of which hit Ricci in the thigh. She threw the third at him before he knew what hit him the first time.

He brought his rifle up, recognized Katie, and then he smiled.

"Shoot him, Todd!" Katie yelled.

Todd took careful aim and hit a tree.

They both ducked when Ricci returned fire. Katie's eyes narrowed on Todd. "You did it. You missed the side of a barn . . ."

"Coax him out and I'll take another shot," Todd whispered.

"Are you crazy? You coax him out and I'll shoot him."

"No," he told her, reloading the gun. "He'll kill me but he won't kill you." He snapped the cartridge shut.

"Katie?" Ricci's rich voice called from out of the trees. With the echo, he sounded near, too near. "I don't want to hurt you. Come out and I'll let your brother live."

They stared at each other. "How does he know I'm your brother?" Todd whispered.

"Nadine, I guess, but let's try again. I'll throw another rock." Together they peered out from behind the boulder. She could not see Ricci but heard his voice as if he were standing beside her.

"If I have to force you out, I'll kill Todd. I'll take my skinning knife and gut him like a trout."

Katie jerked her head around and screamed when Ricci ran straight for her. Todd had no time to swing the pistol toward him.

Ricci's hands felt like steel when he grabbed her by the shoulders.

Todd took careful aim.

"Shoot me. Go ahead young man, but make sure you don't hit your little sister."

"Katie," Todd mouthed, taking a step toward her.

Ricci adjusted his hold on her neck, keeping himself shielded.

"You need a doctor. Your shoulder will become infected and you'll lose that arm if you're not treated." Todd lowered the gun and took another step toward them. "I can look after you. I have medicine in my saddlebag."

Ricci backed away, dragging Katie with him. "I don't

need a doctor. I need a nurse." His nose touched Katie's cheek.

Todd stared at her. She saw his desperation and his desire to rescue her.

"Time to die, Doctor." Ricci took quick aim but before he pulled the trigger, Todd jumped and rolled out of the way. Ricci fired again but Todd had ducked safely behind the boulder.

Ricci all but threw Katie into the saddle and mounted behind her. Injured or not, his muscles gripped her like granite. He kicked the horse into a full gallop toward the south and then eastward. They rode for long while and Katie tried to calm herself. *Think,* she told herself. *Think!* She had to get away from him.

But where was Murphy? Was Buck dead? Was Murphy?

A sick feeling churned in her stomach. Ricci held her so tightly that she struggled to breathe. She did not know where they headed or even in which direction they rode. The sun stayed hidden behind the cloud covering. Wind fanned the pine trees. Riding uphill, Katie saw jagged rocks along the hillside.

Pulling in the horse, Ricci slid from the saddles and pulled Katie down with him. He slapped the horse on the rump. Taking Katie by the arm, he dragged her toward the rocks. An opening in the stones revealed a large cave and he shoved her inside.

He had been in the cave previously, for a dugout pit held firewood. Ricci lit a match on the sole of his boot and tossed it into the kindling. Katie watched the wood catch fire and waited for him to make his move.

He walked toward her in a deliberate manner. "You're quite the actress, little Katie." Removing his vest, he tossed it aside. "I thought you wanted the sheriff dead. Well, you got your wish. His body is lying at the bottom of a canyon."

"I don't believe you."

He put out his bottom lip. "Oh, see there, you've hurt my feelings again." Without touching her, he leaned in and spoke in a rumbling tone, "Who do you love, Katie, more than anyone?"

Murphy came to her mind. She would have to see his lifeless body to believe such a man would die and leave her here with Ricci.

Ricci kept pace as Katie slid along the wall. "I think you love yourself, I think you do. You thought you were so clever at the cabin, didn't you?" He rambled wildly and Katie wondered if the pain put him out of his mind. "You are a clever girl. And as attractive as that is to me I'm going to have to tame your spirit." He pulled a knife from his belt as his black eyes studied her features. "You're too pretty for you own good." Cold steel touched Katie's cheek and the tip of the knife pierced to draw blood. "A long scar might tame you."

Wildly frantic, Katie defended herself. She seized his wounded leg and twisted with all her might.

He screamed and pulled backward. "You've a lot of hatred and vengeance in you, Katie. You really are the perfect woman for me." He lunged for her.

Kicking, screaming, punching, and writhing, Katie landed on her back anyway with Ricci leaning over her.

She twisted away from him and landed on her belly with her face near the fire.

Ricci whipped her around and straddled her. He did not see the flaming stick of wood she had plucked from the blaze.

Katie hit Ricci with the torch until his shirtsleeve caught fire.

Shouting in pain, he rolled into the dirt to put out the flame. Then he jumped to his feet.

Katie stood too and held the torch threateningly.

Hatred smoldered in those black eyes. His upper lip curled into a sneer. He had developed a tick along his left cheek and eyelid. "Drop it or I'll shoot you." He pulled a derringer from the back of his belt and aimed it at her.

Katie lifted the flame above her head. "Shoot me, Anthony. I'd rather die than be with you." She did not really want to die. That was why she threw the torch straight at Ricci face before he took his shot.

He raised his arm to block the attack and then fell against the wall. The flame missed him, but his wounded leg slowed him as he tried to stand again.

Katie ran for the cave opening and once outside she sprinted downslope and then horizontally along the hill toward the trees. She heard Ricci behind her.

Naggy stood near a cluster of pines. Katie slowed to keep from spooking the animal. She searched the saddle and tried to remove the large rifle in the scabbard. She meant to mount but Ricci's arm went around her waist as he dragged her away from the horse.

She held tight to the horn of the saddle. Her hands found a water bottle and gripped it. The metal canteen came loose when the horse reared. Katie twisted around and hit Ricci in the face with it.

He had holstered his pistol and now used both hands to protect himself.

When he made another grab for her waist, Katie wrapped the canteen strap around his throat. She squeezed the leather and then pulled hard until Ricci had to use both his hands to claw at the strap.

Bending toward her, Ricci wrestled with the leather. Finally, he kicked Katie's legs out from beneath her, and then kicked her hard in the thigh.

She released the strap and rolled away from him, then quickly getting to her feet, she ran. She traveled upslope thinking to keep things difficult for Ricci. Beaten, burned, shot, knifed, and strangled ought to slow a man down!

Ricci's hand snatched the material of Katie's blouse and collar, but she kept running. The material ripped at the seam.

She landed on her hands and knees and crawled away from him. The palms of her hands found pebbles and Katie twisted around to throw them at his face. When the pebbles ran out, she flung dirt into his eyes.

That stopped him momentarily and she got to her feet again. Realizing that Ricci was temporarily blind, Katie pushed him hard in the chest and he fell backward down the slope.

She took off uphill.

A bullet grazed the bark of a tree to her right and she hit the ground front first. Crawling again, she made for the boulder three feet away. The slab became her goal.

It was two feet away. Another bullet glanced off the boulder and Katie froze. Ducking her face beneath her arm, she peeked out to see that Ricci pointed the barrel straight at her.

She rolled left, and then right.

Ricci pulled the trigger again and a bullet pinged off the ground where Katie had lain a moment before. She stopped moving, waiting for the next bullet to tear open her backside.

A rumbling sound came from her left.

Opening her eyes, Katie saw the big cat crouched behind the boulder. The cougar's narrowed eyes glared at Katie; its neb wrinkled, exposing long and sharp fangs. Then it screamed in outrage.

Katie pushed to her feet and ran straight for Ricci.

The cat bounded off the hill after her.

Ricci took in the situation in an instant. He pulled the trigger and the cougar's scream was cut short. Ricci shot it again.

Katie kept running all the way down the hill and straight into Big Buck's waiting arms.

"We meet again," he said pleasantly and shoved her behind him in a protective manner. He pulled a small knife from his boot. "Ricci up there?"

"Ricci and a cougar."

"Well, ain't that a pretty pair." He took a step forward. Katie stepped with him, clinging to the back of his vest.

Murphy heard gunfire and moved in the same direction. He cut upslope and then eastward. At the same time he watched Todd and Sawbones race along the forest floor beneath him. Where was Katie? Were the gunshots meant for her? His heart jerked to a fast pace but he tried to calm his thoughts. Knowing the girl as well as he did now, he thought she might be the one shooting all the bullets.

The cougar lay dead on the ground and Ricci walked down the hill toward Buck and Katie. Pistol drawn, he smiled at the bartender. "You're still out here? I thought you'd be back at your bar drinking all the profits." He loaded the gun as he walked toward them.

"You should've finished the job when you had the chance," Buck told him, pushing Katie away. "Of course, with the way you aim, there ain't much chance of you hitting me."

"Oh, but there's such an enormous chance now." Ricci cocked the derringer.

Buck raised the knife, fisting it so that it became a true menace. "I'll have your liver in a jar over my bar." He circled Ricci. "You may get a shot off but know this: One bullet won't stop me."

Ricci grinned at the man's audacity. "One bullet in the brain will stop you."

"If I had a brain," Buck replied loudly and joyfully.

Katie saw Naggy running straight toward Buck after hearing his voice. The horse came from the left side of the trees and nearly trampled her and pushed her toward Ricci.

Ricci and Buck both stared in surprised at the animal's appearance. It gave Ricci the diversion he needed to run and grab Katie around the neck with his forearm. He cocked the pistol when he pushed the barrel on her temple.

Buck grabbed the buffalo gun from the scabbard and jacked a shell into the chamber.

"Back away," Ricci warned, shoving the cold metal hard against Katie's head. "Don't doubt that I will shoot her." His arm went from her throat to her waist and he took a step backward. "She said she'd rather die than be with me. I'll make her wish come true."

Buck sighted the rifle and stepped toward them. Before he took another step, Ricci jerked Katie around to the right.

Sheriff Wade Murphy stood five yards away with his pistol drawn. His eyes were like cold steel and they held a threat impossible to ignore.

Ricci faltered and then screamed, "You can't have her, Sheriff! She is coming with me. I won't let you take her. I'll kill her first."

Murphy brought the pistol level and took aim. He did not blink; he did not appear to breathe at all. His finger started to squeeze the trigger.

Ricci took the pistol from Katie's head and pointed the gun at the sheriff. He pulled the trigger but the bullet went wild and into the trees.

The bullet from Murphy's pistol exploded out of the chamber and hit Ricci in the middle of his face.

Katie fell to the ground with him. She would not look to see Ricci's dead body lying next to her. Then Murphy was there and he scooped her into his arms.

She trembled all over and might have collapsed but Murphy spoke gently to her and brushed the hair from her face. "You're hurt," he said, eyeing the blood on her cheek.

Katie shook her head. "I don't care." And she didn't. Ricci lay dead and she was free of him at last.

"Well, I care," he said, helping her sit up.

"I guess we ought to bury him," Buck said. He stood out of Katie's view.

"I'll send some men back from Victor," Murphy told him. "The undertaker will bury him."

"I meant the cougar," Buck explained, coming around to kneel beside Katie. "Ricci can rot where he lies for all I care. I'm happy to see that you are still breathing, Miss Thomas."

"Thanks to both of you," Katie told him and gazed at Murphy. "Buck was very courageous. He told Ricci that he would cut out his liver and display it in a jar over his bar."

The big man's face broke into a wide grin. "Sorry ma'am. I shouldn't have said that, what with your gentle upbringing and all."

Todd, just arriving, scoffed at the words. Dismounting Sawbones, he brought a medical kit to Katie's side. "Gentle upbringing? What's he talking about, Katie?"

Lightning licked the top of the mountain. The wind gusts carried the scent of rain. Pine trees and oaks moaned with the relentless blowing. Surely, the hounds of hell came for Ricci's soul. Lengthening shadows, like long dark fingers, grabbed for him as the sun disappeared completely behind the thunderclouds. Any moment now, Katie would see Ricci's spirit led down the slope to a bottomless pit.

With Katie on her feet again, the men moved toward the horses standing nearby. She stayed near Todd as her uneasiness grew. She did not understand her feelings. Anthony was dead. She should feel relief. Yet the approaching storm and the rumbling thunder disturbed her deep down inside, far out of reach, down in a place farther than her memory. The long shadows on the ground not only reached for Anthony, they reached for Katie as well.

She saw Murphy ahead of her. He studied the sky and the clouds boiling and tumbling over each other. "We need to find shelter," he called to Buck. "There isn't time to get to town."

Katie's heart sank. She did not want to stay there when the storm broke. It was too similar to another place and time.

"Should we build shelter?" Todd asked. He shoved at his glasses and the wind tossed his blond hair.

"This devil-wind would make firewood out of a lean-to," Buck told him. "Let's try to find a cave instead." He moved toward the rocks.

Murphy came to stand in front of Katie and offered her his hands. "Stay with me." His eyes watched her face and studied the cut on her cheek. When she took his hands, his eyes came back to hers. What did he see there that caused him such concern? His brow creased and his eyes narrowed. "Are you all right?"

She tried to smile. "I don't like the storm. Can we try to get to town?" She moved closer to him.

"We can't make it."

He did not understand that she could not stay there. He did not know the raging emotion she experienced down in the pit of her stomach. It cut off the breath in her throat. "Please?" When he only watched her, Katie grew angry. She would leave them all and head to town by herself!

"Katie? Are you listening to me?"

"NO!" she screamed, and tried to snatch her hands from his. "I want to go home."

"I told you, there's no time."

She wrenched free of him and hurried toward the horses.

Murphy stopped her and swung her around. "You'll stay with us."

When a bolt of lightning hit the ground and thunder cracked right above them, Katie bent at the waist and covered her ears. She would have screamed but Murphy snatched her by the shoulders and dragged her close.

She would not look at him.

Murphy held her at arm's length. "Do you remember the last storm you were in, Katie? The wind blew like this and the lightning struck close."

She grew more agitated as he spoke. What did he hope to do, force her to remember what happened?

She would not! Fear closed in around her and rose like a thick cloud to leave an acrid taste in her mouth. She pushed Murphy away and ran toward the horses again. She managed to get her boot into one stirrup.

Murphy's arm encircled her waist and hauled her backward. "You can't leave!"

"I hate you, Murphy. I swear, I hate you." She beat her fist against his chest. She would have kicked and bit him but some small piece of her brain remembered that she loved him and did not want to hurt him. "Let me go."

"I won't. Not until you tell me what's scaring you."

"I want to go home," she shrieked, still trying to push out of his grip. "Why won't you take me home?" Hot tears stung her cheeks. "You'll make me suffer just to get your money. You're as bad as Anthony Ricci."

Murphy pulled back from her as though she had physically slapped him. "I want to help you. You're frightened."

She continued to lash out at him; she did not want him to ever bring up this subject again and she thought to make it clear forever. "All you care about is being right, Sheriff."

"Over here," Buck called to them. "There's a cave on the other side of the rocks."

"We'll talk about this later," Murphy told her angrily. He pulled her along beside him.

Buck pointed to the opening in the rocks. "Fire wood is lit. Ricci must have stayed here."

Katie stopped short, unable to enter the cave.

Murphy tried to pull her inside. "Come on, Katie."

"I can't . . . I can't go in there."

"Why not?" His blue eyes were narrow slits of ice.

She answered in a calm voice. "Go ahead inside. I'll wait out here." She moved toward an overhang.

Todd paused at the opening.

Buck stuck his head out. "There's nothing in here but a fire."

Katie shook her head.

Murphy tried to drag her but she fought him.

Todd touched Murphy's arm. "I'll stay out here with Katie. You two go on inside."

Buck followed him out of the cave. "I never liked caves myself."

The shelf in the rocks turned out to be no shelter at all when the wind threw the hail at them and the trees nearly bent over and slapped them. Katie stood between Murphy and Todd. Thunder boomed and lightning flashed all around them. It sounded like dynamite exploding. Streams of light blinded her even though she kept her eyelids tightly closed. When she peeked out into the trees, puddles of fire scorched the ground and the smell of voltage filled the air. The horses whinnied and bumped into each other.

It remained dark until the next bolt hit and the woodland lit up like an inferno, blinding her again. Someone grabbed her around the waist to comfort her but when another strike hit close, Katie screamed. She did not know where Murphy stood anymore. She did not know where Todd stood. She fell to her knees to scream and scream and scream.

The lightning danced up the other side of the mountain and rain came in sheets. Thunder roared. Todd and Murphy threw nervous glances at each other. Katie's screaming unnerved them.

Todd fell at Katie's side and put his arm around her.

When she did not stop screaming, Murphy put his arm around her as well and then Big Buck moved to kneel in front of her. They meant to fight the unseen assailant, but it was in her mind.

"Katie," Todd shouted over the noise of the pounding rain. He grabbed her upper arms. "KATIE!"

She opened her eyes and stared at him. He looked scared and shook her hard. "STOP IT."

Murphy broke his grasp. "Leave her alone."

Katie lifted her hands to cover her face. Realizing where she was, and understanding the worst of the storm had past, she tried to stand.

Murphy watched her as she blinked rainwater from her eyes. What had happened? She had obviously done something wrong. She could tell it by the looks on their faces. "What's the matter?" she asked.

"You screamed," Murphy told her.

Was that all? "The lightning was so close."

The sheriff nodded and then stared at Todd.

Katie's eyes followed Murphy's.

Todd spit out, "For crying out loud, Katie. You scared me to death." Angry, he spun away from her to find his horse. Though it still poured, he grabbed Sawbones' reins with vengeance. "Let's get out of here."

Murphy kept hold of Katie's arm. "She can ride with me."

"She'll ride with me," Todd snapped. He grabbed her wrist and pulled her forward. Pushing her into the saddle, he swung up behind her. They moved toward the trail when Todd's grip tightened.

Katie tried to push his arm away and at last hollered

for him to stop. When he wouldn't, she lifted her leg over the horse's neck to dismount, but her brother grabbed her by the shoulders before she jumped. "Todd, you're hurting me!"

His eyes hardened dangerously. She had never seen him so angry. "Why did you do that, Katie? What's the matter with you?" He held on even though she struggled hard.

When at last he released her, Katie fell from the horse but landed on her feet.

Todd followed her down.

Buck dismounted quickly and stepped between brother and sister. "What do you think you're doing? Let her be."

Murphy dismounted too. He grabbed Todd by the arm. "She is okay, Todd. She's fine. The lightning scared her, that's all."

"That isn't all, Murphy. You can't think her reaction is normal." He pulled away from Murphy's hand. "She must tell me what the matter is so that I can help her."

"But you're not helping her," Murphy shouted. "Yelling at her won't make her remember any faster."

Todd's eyes were red-rimmed and angry. He pushed his glasses onto his nose and took a deep breath. Wiping his brow, he stared at Buck. "Sorry, old buddy," he told him and then, "Katie? Katie, I'm sorry. You scared me. Please come here."

He did not need to ask again. Katie fell into his arms.

Chapter Nine

Two days later, Katie sat at the vanity in her bedroom and pulled the sides of her hair into a French Twist. The scratches on her cheeks had healed quickly, except the cut, but her complexion looked pale. Dark circles smudged her blue eyes. Sleep stalked her, yet she would not give into it. The dreams would come again. She could not remember what the dreams entailed but it became so that she dreaded nightfall. The night before she had left a candle burning at her bedside to chase the nightmares away. They came anyway, waking her suddenly, and leaving her in a cold sweat.

Todd called to Katie from downstairs. He wanted her to talk to Ben Raines that morning and she grew uneasy. Talking to the man would dredge up memories best left alone.

Ben came fully awake the day before. Todd interviewed him, but Katie avoided the conversation. If she were not so tired, she would have the strength for it.

"Katie," Todd called again.

She smoothed the skirt of her pale blue dress and took the stairs.

It had been two days since she had seen Murphy as he had been busy squaring away the details of Ricci's death and contacting the New York prison and Anthony's next of kin.

When she spotted him at the bottom of the stairs, her heart skipped a beat and she brightened. He'd had his hair cut and the soft brown waves fell on the sides of his face. The back of it had been cut above the collar of his white shirt. His gray-blue eyes never left Katie as she descended the stairs and he held out his hand for her to take. Then he kissed her cheek affectionately. "You look beautiful," he whispered.

Katie colored at his words and at his nearness. "Not too much dark circling around my eyes?" she asked, grinning at him. She stood on the bottom step to stay eye level with him.

"It would take more than dark rings to ruin your beauty."

"Barlett Sanders."

Murphy shook his head. "Nope. I have decided you aren't the girl for me."

She heard what he said but his eyes told her differently. "Really?"

"Yup."

She placed her hands on his solid shoulders. "I know why too. It's because I can outshoot you."

"Oh, it is not."

"That shot you took at Ricci? I could've done it at twice the distance."

He yawned to show her how bored he was with the argument and he took a step backward.

Katie held on to him. "It bothers you, doesn't it? You can tell me."

Todd cleared his throat from the door of the middle office. "If you two are ready, Ben is in here."

Ben Raines sat on the examination table. His shirt hung opened to reveal a white bandage across his chest. He pushed his light brown hair off his forehead and then his mouth broke into a wide smile when he gazed at Katie.

She knew an immediate kinship with the man. Their shared disaster bonded them somehow. He said, "Katie Thomas, it's good to see you again."

He sounded so sincere that she walked toward the table and took his outstretched hands. "I'm happy that you're feeling better."

Todd stood beside the counter with a merry look on his face and he pushed his glasses onto his nose. "I've filled Ben in on what's been happening since the stage robbery." He spoke to Katie then, "I thought you and Murphy would like to hear his version of what went on that day."

Katie looked at Murphy, who leaned one hip against the wall cabinet. He raised a brow at her and nodded in encouragement.

"Todd told me that you don't remember much," Ben said. "Do you remember our last stop in Lincoln when we picked up a man named Hank Walker?" Katie shook her head and Ben continued. "I was sorry to put him back in the cab with you. It made it crowded with the professor, that actor fellow Moon, and Foster Garrett, but you said you would be fine so we drove on."

His words came slower and he stared at the wall as he recalled the journey. "We were about a mile away from Victor City and I heard a gunshot inside the cab. We pulled on the reins when all of a sudden more shots sounded. They came from beside us on the right. I let the horses run and the ride got rough." He pushed at his hair again. "I thought about you being tossed around back there in the cab, Katie, but I couldn't help you."

An image of trees speeding by the cab door flashed through Katie's memory.

"Darryl rode shotgun and returned fire but he got hit and fell from the coach." The loss of his friend clearly affected Ben and he sat for a moment without saying anything.

Katie squeezed his hand. She should not have dreaded talking to Ben. He was just as traumatized as she was.

He cleared his throat. "Anyway, I was concerned for you because of the gunfire inside the coach, but it was the dandiest thing. When I looked over my shoulder, you were hanging on to the side of the coach. I don't know how you got out of the cab unless you fell out of the door that swung open."

"Oh, it makes perfect sense if you know my sister," Todd interjected and grinned at Katie.

Ben waited politely before continuing. "A bullet hit me. It jabbed into my shoulder like a hot poker. I glanced back and saw Hank Walker aiming to hit me again. He reached for you . . . you fell, Katie."

She looked at her brother. "That's how I stood and saw what happened."

Todd nodded at her. "That makes sense."

"It was a wild ride," Ben continued. "We tore off the trail and all I remember seeing were the trees zipping by on every side." He gazed at Katie again. "I remember falling. The coach must have crashed and I stared into the pine trees and at the sky. A storm brewed there." He had a faraway look again as he thought on the point. He blinked rapidly and said to Katie, "Then you were there, like an angel."

Todd groaned, "Oh, brother."

Katie threw him a look and then turned to Ben. "Go on," she told him. "I looked like a heavenly angel."

Ben chuckled. "Yes, but I heard horses coming at us from the south. I told you to take the moneybag and run."

Vindication at last, thought Katie, and she looked at Murphy.

Murphy shrugged. "I knew you were innocent the moment I laid eyes on you, Katie Thomas."

"He arrested me," Katie told Ben.

"Murphy?" Ben tried to turn around to see the sheriff but could not quite make it around that far.

Murphy pushed off the wall to stand near Ben. "There were other reasons why I arrested her. She sneaked into your room when I told her to stay away from you."

"That doesn't sound too criminal to me."

Murphy asked, "Can you remember anything else?"

"No, after I gave Katie my pistol, I must've passed out."

"You gave her a pistol?"

"Sure," Ben told him. "I gave her my silver-plated Remington, why?" He glanced at Katie again. "Did you lose it?"

"I don't remember it," she told him slowly. But then, all the sudden she did. She remembered leaning over Ben and taking the pistol from him. She said, "I ran east."

"Yes," Ben agreed. "I told you to run east so that you could get back to the Overland Trail."

Murphy's eyes narrowed. "So you did take Hank's gun from him, just as I thought. The pistols got switched . . ." He turned to Katie. "Think a minute. Did you drop the pistol or the moneybag? Did you try to hide the money?"

"Katie," Todd said when she was slow to answer. "Do you recall any of this?" He wanted her to remember and she hated to disappoint him. Todd had fussed over her ever since they had returned home. It seemed as though he were trying to make up for his actions during the lightning storm after Ricci died.

She wanted to tell them something, anything. "I remember you, Ben. I recall that you gave me your pistol and I started to run. Trees blew over . . ."

"What else?" Todd urged her.

Katie shook her head. "I don't know."

Frustrated, he replied, "Come on, think. It stormed. Lightning flashed, thunder cracked overhead, and you ran. What happened next?"

Katie's stomach tightened as he spoke. His words scared her and then anger rose in fear's place. "I told you that I don't remember." She regretted showing her temper when Todd's face turned pale. If he would only stop acting so anxious over her, she would feel less pressure. "I'm sorry," she told all of them and started to leave the room.

Murphy blocked the door. "Wait. Just sit a minute." He gazed at Katie and then smiled gently.

Katie shook her head. She would not sit. Before he asked any questions, she said, "I can't think of anything else."

"It's all right," he soothed. "Hank Walker followed you. We know that." His hand reached for her elbow and when she tried to move away, he took her other arm to make her face him. "He tried to take the money from you."

Katie wanted to cry. When would he stop asking so much of her?

Suddenly his arms closed in around her and Murphy held her tightly to his chest. "It's all right," he repeated.

But it was not all right. Nothing would ever be right again.

"Do you have something to calm her?" Murphy asked over her head.

Katie pulled away. "I don't want anything."

"It'll help you sleep," Todd told her, already pulling open a drawer. She must have looked wild because suddenly he stopped and stared at her. "You haven't been sleeping. I know you haven't."

Katie struggled out of Murphy's arms and backed away from him. She would not look at him or Ben or even at her brother. "He comes at night."

"Who comes at night?" Murphy asked.

She did not explain and found the door handle. Todd called to her but she did not turn around.

Murphy stopped her on the first stair. She thought he would ask her to remember more, but he didn't. He said, "The circuit judge is in town and has requested an examination of everyone involved in the case. He would like to meet after lunch. I hate to insist."

A tight feeling grabbed her stomach. She didn't want to talk to the judge. She didn't want to talk to anyone. The issue needed to die and the best way for it to do that was to forget it completely.

"It's a formality, Katie. There's nothing to it."

"Then why must I attend?" She refused to look at him and studied the button on the top of his shirt.

"You were jailed. We have to clear your name."

"If you hadn't arrested me in the first place I wouldn't have to have my name cleared."

"I'm sorry." His voice sounded husky and it caused Katie to look into his eyes. "I am sorry."

She was not angry with Murphy, not really. She was just so exhausted. Trying to explain, she said, "I want to put it all behind me."

"We will, I promise. The judge must hear the facts of the case before that'll happen, though."

She lifted her shoulder weakly.

"I'll come for you after lunch," Murphy told her. "I'll

stay with you through the whole procedure and I'll even hold your hand if you like." He took a step backward. "Try to rest. I'll come for you soon."

Murphy's office served as the courtroom. The honorable Calvin Mitchell thumped his gavel. "We are assembled here to acknowledge and sign death certificates, issue handbills, clear Kathryn Rebeccah Thomas' name since she endured incarceration, and to state once and for all that murder is not the answer to every one of life's sticky problems." Mitchell laughed at his own joke and took a sip of water from a glass on Murphy's desk. He spoke to a slight man keeping record. "In attendance: Sheriff Wade Murphy, Kathryn Thomas, Dr. Todd Thomas, Maurice "Big Buck" Lamar, Benjamin Raines, Mr. Theodore Welch of the Victor City Bank, and Charles Nottington, coroner, gravedigger, and casket maker."

Charlie Ghoul, Katie remembered.

"I hereby bring this court to order and the first business is . . ." He flipped through the mound of paperwork. "The dead: Darryl Jones, Hank Walker, Theodore Moon, James Caldwell, Anthony Ricci, and Foster Garrett. I now sign these death certificates and you are all witness to my action."

Once the judge finished signing, he handed the papers to Murphy, who signed them and then handed them to Charles Nottington.

Katie twisted her gloved hands in her lap and took steady breaths to keep her dizzy feeling in check.

Mitchell continued, "I am setting forth a handbill

for the arrest of Jake Cherry for . . ." He glanced at Murphy.

"Intending to shoot an officer of the law, kidnapping, stage robbery, and attempted murder," Murphy replied.

"A five hundred dollar reward is set forth for the delightful Mr. Cherry." After writing the number, the judge peered at the assembly through his small glasses. "All right, who shot Anthony Ricci?"

Murphy raised his index finger. As promised, he sat next to Katie. He still wore his white shirt, which caused his skin to look bronzed.

Judge Mitchell shook his head. "Too bad, Murphy. You're not eligible for the five hundred dollar reward."

"I believe it was my bullet that got him," Buck chimed in, glancing at the sheriff for support. "We were both aiming at him."

"Your buffalo gun would have shattered his whole face," Charlie Ghoul put in and then shrank back in his chair when the bartender glared at him.

The judge hammered the gavel, this time finding wood to make noise with it. "Maurice, there are certain ramifications for lying in my courtroom." He shuffled his papers. He was at least fifty years old and had gray hair and dark eyes behind his spectacles. He wore a black brocade vest and a blue jacket overtop it. Mitchell glanced at Ben Raines. "How are you feeling, young man? Able to sit up and take nourishment, are you?"

"I am healing, Your Honor."

"Who shot you?"

"Hank Walker."

The judge looked at his secretary and the man answered, "Dead."

Mitchell gazed around the room. "So that brings us to Kathryn Thomas." He smiled kindly but Katie's stomach took a plunge. Murphy grabbed her gloved hand into his and his thumb rubbed at the lace there. The judge asked her, "Who did you shoot?"

Taken aback, Katie stared at him.

Murphy cleared his throat and sat forward in his chair. "We believe she shot Hank Walker."

The gavel pounded. "Eight hundred dollars is awarded to Kathryn—"

"I don't want it." She stared at Murphy. "I don't want any money."

He nodded and looked at the judge again. "She's not convinced she killed the man."

Mitchell narrowed his eyes on her. "Did you point a gun at him and pull the trigger?"

Katie shook her head.

Todd stood and approached the desk. "She has forgotten the day, Your Honor, the worst part of it, anyway. She needs time to recover."

Mitchell rubbed his nose where his glasses sat. "Hold the reward money until Kathryn's memory returns to her." When he opened his eyes, he stared at Ben again. "Now, Mr. Raines, where's the money due the Victor City Bank?"

"Lost, Your Honor."

"By lost you mean stolen?"

"No, I mean lost. I gave the money to Katie and she can't remember where she put it."

Judge Mitchell's eyes swung back to her. "You *gave* the money to her?"

"Yes. Thieves came to steal it so I gave it to Katie and told her to run."

Faded eyes narrowed and glared at the stage driver. "That was a foolish mistake, Mr. Raines. The bank and the stage line may make case against you for misman-agement of their property."

Mr. Welch stood then. "Victor City Bank won't press charges, Your Honor. Mr. Raines risked his life to pro-tect it."

"No, he risked Kathryn's life," snapped Mitchell.

Katie would not allow Ben to take responsibility for the matter and she stood to approach the desk.

Murphy stood with her. Then Todd came to his feet, as did Big Buck. Charlie Ghoul appeared confused and then pushed out of his seat to join the crowd. Katie said, "Our lives were already at risk, sir, and Mr. Raines lay dying. His last thought was to protect the bank's money and to protect me. He's an honorable man. Please don't accuse him of wrongdoing on my account."

Calvin Mitchell nodded. "Very well. Will everyone sit down, please?" Once accomplished, the judge frowned at Ben Raines. "Though you are an honorable man, Ben, you may lose your job."

"That'll be just fine." He spoke while smiling at Katie. "I like it here in Victor City."

Sheriff Murphy shifted in his chair to glare at Ben. "You may like it farther west."

"I may not."

"Order," the judge interrupted. "Now, Miss Thomas, you were jailed for . . ." He studied his papers. "Shooting Hank Walker."

"Which you just gave her a reward for doing," Todd reminded him.

"It says here that you entered Ben Raines room . . ."

Ben spoke up. "I'll drop those charges, sir."

"You didn't make the charges."

"I never complained, either."

"Miss Thomas is charged with leaving town?" Mitchell asked Murphy.

"Can those be dropped with the suspicion of murder and robbery charges?" Murphy asked, leaning forward again.

The judge removed and then dropped his glasses onto the pages. "All charges are dropped against Kathryn Thomas. If there is no other order of business, I will close this case."

Murphy got to his feet. "I'd like to leave the case open for another month."

"Why?" Mitchell asked.

Exactly, Katie thought. Why?

"Because the money is still missing."

Katie's teeth came together. Finding the money certainly was his biggest concern.

Murphy's eyes found hers and he hunkered in front of her chair. "We need to finish this, Katie. You know we have to clear everything."

Without a word, Katie looked away to stare at the judge.

Mitchell said, "Very well, I'll hear your findings in a month, Sheriff. Right now, however, this court is adjourned."

Murphy caught up to Katie on the porch. The rest of the men were in the yard and walking to the gate and toward the main road. Todd still stood at Katie's side, but after catching Murphy's eyes, he too stepped off the porch.

Katie did not want to talk to the sheriff and moved off the steps.

Murphy blocked the way. "Have dinner with me tonight?"

"No," she told him. "You'll want to talk about the money."

"We won't talk about it tonight." When she did not answer, he leaned on the step's railing and tilted his head. In the late sunshine, his brown hair showed a hint of red in it and his eyes appeared more gray than blue. "Come on, Katie. Have dinner with me and I'll stay on my best behavior."

It was too hard to resist the man. "You have to promise . . ."

Murphy held up his right hand. "I swear to treat you in a respectable manner due a woman who can shoot worth a nickel and who can cook a mean meat stew." When she only smiled, he asked, "Deal?"

She sighed and looked toward the telegraph office. "Deal."

Murphy fit the Stetson onto his head and bowed in a

gallant fashion. "Good day, then. I'll see you at dinner-time."

"Good-bye," she whispered and watched him walk into his office again.

Murphy and Katie ate at Marigold's Kitchen. The only other restaurant in town was at Blue Bells and it had a smaller dining room. The town of Chicago had many more amenities. She would return there soon but that night she wanted to enjoy Wade Murphy. He dressed differently than she had seen him before—gray slacks and a white shirt with a gray tie under a black jacket. He looked handsome and charming and quite at ease. He pushed his plate away. "What are you thinking about, Katie?"

"That we sat at this same table the first time we met."

Murphy glanced around the room. "I guess we did." His eyes came back to hers. "I'll tell you what I should've told you that day. You're the prettiest girl on earth."

"You told me that later."

"Right. Well, I meant it."

She grinned at him. "*No,* you tried to manipulate me like a point man would."

"Right. Well, I still meant it."

"Murphy, have you seen every girl on earth?"

"Maybe not all of them but I've seen plenty in Denver."

Todd had told Katie that Murphy grew up in Denver. She asked, "Are your parents still there?"

"My father is and my stepmother."

"What does your father do?"

Murphy took a drink from his water glass. "My father is the mayor of Denver."

"No kidding?"

"No kidding."

"Did you have a sweetheart in school or after school?"

He nodded. "Sure. Her name was Grace Richards. Now it's Grace Tidewell."

"She turned you down for another man, a man named Tidewell?"

"I didn't say . . ."

"Well how in the blue-eyed world did she become Tidewell if she didn't turn you down?"

"I never asked . . ."

"Why not?"

Murphy grimaced. "Because I knew she wasn't the one . . ."

"Wasn't Grace pretty?"

"She was beautiful."

"Did she have good teeth?"

"I guess so. I don't remember!"

Katie gaped at him. "Well, why did you break it off with her?" By the squint of his gray-blue eyes, Katie knew she'd gotten beneath his skin, and she laughed in delight. "Murphy you are so easily provoked."

"Well, you'd provoke anybody!"

"Thank you," she told him demurely.

He smiled at that. "Well, what about you? Did you have a suitor?"

"I went to a women's college, Murphy."

"You didn't like someone in school?"

"His name was Tharius Bethel." She forked her green beans.

"No, it was not."

"That was his name!"

"Well, what sort of name is that?"

"It doesn't matter, Murphy, pay attention. Tharius was in the next grade and he sat in the desk in front of me. I used to stare at the back of his head and just feel so in love."

Murphy looked confused. "With the back of his head?"

"I knew what the front of his head looked like, okay?"

He chuckled. "Go on."

"One day he turned to me and asked if I would go ice-skating with him."

"And you fell in love on the ice?"

"I never liked him after that."

He put his elbow on the table and cupped his chin in his hand. "Why not?"

"Because he couldn't skate and it embarrassed me."

Murphy thought about what she said. "How old were you?"

"Nine, I think."

He dropped his hand onto the table. "You only had one suitor?"

"Of course not. I thought you wanted to hear about the most interesting one."

"That was the most interesting?"

She laughed at his expression. "I'm going to miss you so much, Murphy."

His brows came together. "Miss me? Do you want to return to the jail cell so that you can spend all day with me again?"

With her fork, she pushed at the roast beef on her plate. "No, thank you."

"I'm only across the road and I'll stop in and see you every morning. Maybe you can sing for me. What was it you sang in the basement, 'Nobody Knows the Trouble I've Seen'?"

"I didn't know you were listening."

He leaned his forearms on the edge of the table. "I know." His eyes drifted over her features.

"I bought a ticket to Chicago. I'm leaving the day after tomorrow."

He leaned backward as if he'd been slapped. "What?"

She did not answer, neither did she look at him, but smoothed the napkin in her lap. There was no easy way to tell him except to blurt it out like that. Maybe she shouldn't have told him at all.

"Why, Katie?"

"Because I'm . . ."

"You can't leave."

She met his eyes. "My name is cleared, Murphy. I can go home."

His brows set close and his jaw hardened. "I thought . . ."

He looked genuinely hurt and she explained, "Murphy, I'll never have peace here. This town, you, Buck— everything haunts me. I just want peace. I want to rest."

"*I* haunt you?"

She stared at her plate again. He did not understand.

"You think you can't feel better while you're with me? You're wrong. I'm going to help you. I *can* help you."

Katie shook her head. "If it was possible for a person to stop my nightmares I believe it would be you, Murphy. I've never known anyone as brave and resourceful as you. But I don't think the dreams are going to stop until I get away from here." She smiled at him. "Don't make this harder, Murphy. It's already so hard."

His eyes hardened and he picked up the billing tab. "Do you want to take a walk and get ice cream at Blue Bells?" His voice sounded sharp. Was he angry?

"I think I want to go home."

After he paid for their meal, he held out his arm and walked her across the street. "You leave the day after tomorrow?"

She nodded without looking at him. There were still people milling about even though it was past candle lighting. She heard the piano at Buck's place and a lamp was on in the dressmaker's shop. They stepped into Todd's yard and onto the porch. Murphy pulled her to a stop. "This is wrong, Katie, you know it is."

"Murphy . . ."

He placed his hands on her shoulders and spun her round to look at him. "I don't want you to leave and I don't want to live in Chicago. I've already bought land south of here."

"I didn't ask you to go to Chicago with me." Although she wished with all her heart that he would. Still, she could not imagine Sheriff Wade Murphy in such a place. He belonged here, in the West, in the mountains, taking turns around the town, and arresting the wicked.

He dropped his hands suddenly and backed away. "All right then, Katie. Why don't you try to get some rest? I'll see you tomorrow." He turned and walked toward the road. The way he stepped into the street and walked toward his office had determination to it.

Todd waited for Murphy on the front steps of the sheriff's building. They went inside and Murphy removed his jacket and tie before sitting behind the desk.

"I'm worried about Katie," Todd told him, taking a chair across from him.

Murphy tilted his chair back on two legs. His hands gripped the chair arms and he studied the doctor. They looked alike, Katie and Todd. Their skin tone and eye color were similar and although Todd was much taller, he was slender like Katie.

"She's having nightmares and she wakes troubled every night. When I ask her what she's scared of she tells me it was just a bad dream."

Murphy nodded his head, remembering the night at the cabin when Katie woke terrified and answered the same way. "The day by the stream when we tracked Ricci, she remembered Hank Walker and why she almost shot me."

"She's remembering more than she is telling us?"

"No," he replied. "I thought you said she hit her head. What's going on?"

"I assumed she hit her head because she had so many bruises. I mean, we're still dealing with anterograde amnesia but I think it's trauma induced—psychological and emotional, in other words, not physical." Todd sat back in his chair. "That scares me more than anything else. What happened out there that she's scared to remember?"

"I *know* she shot Hank Walker. She had to, she carried his gun, and she had blood all over the front of her dress when I found her." Murphy ran a hand through his hair and leaned in his chair again, tilting it backward. "But how she came to shoot him is the question."

Todd said what they were both thinking: "He might have attacked her."

Murphy swallowed hard, his heart nearly sat in his throat. His voice sounded strange to his own ears. "You are the doctor, Todd. You examined her. Was there any evidence of it?"

Todd stared out the back door of the office. "I didn't check for that. She had a lot of discoloration and scrapes, which isn't strange if she hung outside the coach as Ben said she did." He stared at Murphy again. "No matter what the horror is, she has to remember it. If she doesn't, I'm scared she'll lose her mind."

"What do you mean?"

"The memory is in the back of her mind and it is affecting other areas of her life. Her reaction to the thunderstorm, the violent dreams every night . . ."

"Saying Hank Walker was a big man and then not remembering she said it to me?"

"Yes, that's what I'm talking about. Do you know she bought a stage ticket for Chicago?"

"Yes," he answered harshly.

"It won't help her to leave. I know you care about her. That's why I came straight over here when I saw you leave the restaurant. We have to do something."

"What?" Murphy knew he would battle Satan to keep Katie sane.

Todd leaned forward. "Katie had the right idea about seeing the place where the stagecoach tipped. Let's take her out there and see if we can shake it out of her."

"We should take her to the spot where I found Hank Walker's body."

"All right."

Murphy thought about it for a minute, knowing it would not be so easy to get Katie out there. If he forced her, would she ever forgive him? He said, "Let me think on it tonight. We'll take her out there tomorrow."

Murphy stood at the back door. He raised a finger to his lips and stared at Barney. "Sit still for a minute while I ask Miss Katie to come with us."

Barney's face broke into a wide grin and he gentled his horse.

"I'll be right back." Murphy opened the screen door to the kitchen and hollered, "Hello?"

Katie stood at the counter wiping canning jars with a cloth. She looked up in surprise. "Wade!"

He grinned at her, pleased at her reaction. She appeared slim and beautiful in a split skirt and knee-high boots. The wide belt she wore caused her waist to look tiny. Murphy liked the way she wore her hair tied up at the sides and let the back of it hang down in waves. He remembered its silky smoothness in his rough fingers. "Is Todd here?" he asked, not caring if Todd was there or not. He could stand and stare at Katie all day and forget why he had come to visit.

Katie regarded Murphy, filling the doorway with his broad shoulders. She wondered if she would ever get over loving him. She moved toward the front room to call for her brother and then stepped toward the counter again to wipe another jar. "Would you like coffee?"

He twirled the Stetson in his hand. "Thank you, no."

"Tea?"

"Offer to come with me this morning."

What the man did to her pulse rate. To think she had once hated him. How could she have ever felt so?

"Barney's waiting outside and we're going to look for the moneybag and Ben's pistol."

His words cut her breath short. The thought of spending her last day in Victor City with Murphy and Barney sounded wonderful, but she hesitated. A deep misery twisted in her belly. A shade of apprehension tightened her chest. Katie exhaled slowly, thinking. "I don't believe I will."

Murphy's brow rose. "You don't want to come along?"

Katie did not want to disappoint him again. "I'm just tired is all, but I'd love to spend time with you and Barney."

"Then come along. I won't make you get out of the carriage if you don't want to."

Katie went to the screen door and stepped past Murphy. Barney sat on Matilda's back as the horse grazed in the mulberry bush. The boy waved to Katie. Katie lifted a hand to wave in return. He was such a happy boy with no cares in the world but trapping, fishing, and hunting. He had a peace about him that Katie wished she could regain.

She turned around and bumped into Murphy's hard chest. He watched her with those blue-gray eyes. Strength lay in the depths and she knew that she trusted him. He took Katie's fingers into his hands and his thumb caressed her palm. "I kept my promise to you last night, Katie. I didn't talk about the moneybag. But it's time to find out what happened out there in the woods." When she started to pull away, Murphy held on tightly. "I swear I'll stay with you. And Barney won't leave your side either."

To stall, Katie asked, "Barney is allowed to be in my company again?"

"I had a long talk with the Crowes. He gets to go with his parents' blessing." When she started to move away again, Murphy put his arm out to block her path. "Come with me."

Powerfully persuaded, Katie knew she would go anywhere with Wade Murphy.

Chapter Ten

They left town. The sun glowed orange in the pale sky and a light breeze cooled her cheeks. Murphy flicked the reins. He sat next to Katie on the buggy bench. Sawbones trotted next to them carrying Todd. Barney rode Matilda on the other side of the carriage and kept Murphy busy in conversation.

Katie did not listen to them. She studied Murphy's profile from the shade of the buggy's canvas. He sat near enough that she saw the tiny lines at the corner of his eyes and the shadow of his beard and mustache.

Barney's voice broke into her thoughts. "Is it true, Miss Katie?"

"Is what true?"

"Did the sheriff save your life again when you escaped Ricci in the cabin?"

Murphy refused to look at her but Katie saw that he

smiled. He clicked his tongue to urge the horse on and slapped the reins gently.

Katie laughed softly. "It's all true, Barney."

Murphy's head snapped up and he sat straighter on the bench—the big phony.

She told Barney, "The sheriff is my hero."

Barney giggled.

Murphy turned his full gaze on Katie when she asked, "Why do you tell the boy such big stories?"

"I did save your life. Well, maybe not at the cabin, but later."

Katie shook her head. "That reminds me of something. Did you tell him you found me running around in the woods all *crazy-like*?"

Murphy looked uncomfortable. He opened his mouth to reply but shut it again. "I don't remember saying *that* precisely."

"Mm-hmm."

Todd and Barney dismounted when they reached the spot where the stagecoach ran off the trail. Murphy halted the buggy and jumped out. He held out his hand to help Katie. "All right," he said, taking charge of the matter. "We've all seen the ruts in the trail." He tossed Katie a smile. "Some of us legally." His hands went to his hips and he said, "We know Katie picked up the moneybag and the pistol and ran east." He walked around the buggy to the opposite side of the trail. "Let's start . . . here."

They walked and Katie enjoyed the outing. She walked with her three favorite men, the sun gleamed overhead, and the birds sang. Maybe they would find the money and the pistol and go home. This nasty business would be over with and tonight she would sleep without nightmares.

Todd caught up with Katie and took her hand as they picked their way through the thicket. "So we are having an adventure."

Katie smiled at him, loving him. "Yes," she agreed. "And most people live and die without having as much adventure in their whole lives as we have had in the last three weeks."

Barney stopped to stare at Katie. "You're so lucky."

Todd and Murphy laughed at him.

The sun rose higher in the sky and it beat down on Katie. She saw the shade of the oak tree and stood at the edge of its shadow, breathing in the coolness. The brightness of the day gave her a headache suddenly and she thought the shade would give relief. If anything, the throbbing grew worse. Her stomach knotted, her chest tightened, and she wondered why she came out here after all. She wished she had stayed home and tried to nap.

Murphy gave instructions. "Fan out and see if we can find the pistol."

Barney moved into the field.

The sun broke through the shade, almost blinding Katie, and she winced. A sharp pain hit her stomach and she nearly bent over from it.

Todd asked, "What's the matter, Katie?"

"Nothing," she told him. "The sun is so bright that it hurts my eyes." She missed the glance Todd threw

Murphy and straightened to take a breath. She could do this, she told herself. "I'll look near the pine trees."

Katie saw Murphy standing beside the oak. He did not look for the pistol. He watched her, waiting for her . . . to do what? She frowned at him.

"Katie Thomas!" he said in a sharp tone.

She hesitated. The sun still blinded her. Even in the shade, she had to cover her eyes for a moment. Her palms grew slick with sweat and her fingers trembled.

"Katie Thomas!" Murphy repeated.

Suddenly she could not breathe. Her stomach rolled. Another flash of light struck her eyes and she closed them tight.

Katie jumped when she heard Barney holler, "I found it, I found it, Sheriff."

She heard the boy's boots crashing through the high grass. Barney ran quickly to Murphy's side and the sun glinted off the weapon he carried . . . lightning flashed, thunder boomed.

"Katie Thomas!" someone yelled behind her. She spun around, no longer able to see Murphy. She saw another man. He was big and barrel-chested. He wore fancy clothing. "Katie Thomas!" the man yelled above the wind. She knew him. By her word, he had gone to prison.

"Give me the money," Hank Walker told her.

"No!" she screamed, lifting her pistol.

He grabbed the gun from her hand and threw it into the field.

Defenseless, she stared at him as he moved toward her. He made to snatch the moneybag but Katie threw it to the ground before he put his hand on it. If he bent to retrieve it, she would run and find the Remington.

His jaw twisted. He stood to his full height and watched her with calculating assessment. "I think you owe me something, Katie Thomas. You stole three months of my life from me."

She said nothing, swallowing back the fear that nearly suffocated her.

He wiped the rain off his top lip with the back of his hand and then he brought the pistol to her face and cocked it. "I think you owe me something . . ." Then he dropped the pistol and reached for her.

Katie did not move fast enough and he grabbed her hair and dragged her backward.

Thunder crashed and the earth shook with it. Lightning danced in agitation.

She twisted and shoved at his chest with all her strength. She kicked and struggled as terror gripped her. She grappled so hard that the man lost his grip and Katie fell to the ground.

Hank Walker laughed at her. He thought she couldn't get away from him. He thought to do whatever he pleased. Taking a step toward her, he leaned down to take hold of the hem of her dress.

Katie clutched at the earth, desperate to find something to stop him—anything, a rock, the moneybag . . . his pistol . . .

The fabric of her skirt tore as he tugged at it.

Katie pointed the gun at his chest and pulled the trigger . . .

Todd's face swam in front of Katie's face. Tears

splashed onto her cheeks like water gushing over rocks. "Did he hurt you?" Todd asked, crying too.

She saw her brother's anguish and touched his face. "No," she whispered. "He tried . . ." She gritted her teeth to say the words Todd needed to hear. "I shot him and his insides sprayed out all over me. It was all over me and he fell on top of me. I couldn't get out from beneath him. He lay on top of me dying, his mouth working, and blood gushing . . . I killed him . . . I KILLED HIM!"

Todd grabbed her hard and held on tight.

Katie saw Murphy. He stood beneath the oak tree and she remembered him that day too. She pushed away from Todd. "I grabbed the moneybag and hid it." She went to the eastern side of the oak and found the knot. She pulled at it twice to dislodge the sack and then shoved it at Murphy's chest.

He said nothing and Katie did not look at his face. "I saw you coming, Sheriff. I didn't know who you were and I thought you must have been with Hank. You called my name as he had called my name and I thought you would try to hurt me too. I swear I meant to kill you."

Murphy nodded. "I know."

Her tears came again. She could not stop them if she tried. With them came all the agony, the torture, and the wretchedness of watching the man die, the man she had killed. Someone pulled her into their arms.

Todd kept Barney at a distance. They walked away from the oak tree and from Katie and Murphy. They threw rocks to keep their minds balanced. Todd never heard Katie cry like that. No woman should ever cry like that. He wanted to be the one who comforted her, but it was Murphy's turn these days. Murphy would protect her.

"Is Miss Katie going to be all right?" Barney wanted to know. Tears gathered in his eyes too and Todd hugged the boy. Barney was an instrument in Katie's healing and Todd wanted him to know it.

"Thank you, Barney. It was a great thing you did today. You helped Miss Katie to feel better."

"She feels better?" he asked skeptically.

Todd smiled. "Believe it or not, she does." He knelt in the tall grass in front of the boy. "She had to remember what happened to her. If she didn't, it would eat her up inside."

Barney understood. "Like consumption?"

Todd nodded and was glad the boy had captured the idea.

"My uncle died of consumption."

"This ate at Katie's insides too, but it won't anymore. You helped when you found the pistol."

Barney grinned.

"I'm grateful to you. With your help, Miss Katie is going to be just fine. I'm sure glad you came with us today."

"Me too!"

After a time, Katie got to her feet. She saw Todd and Barney in the field and she knew Murphy stood at her side but she would not look at him. She never knew such exhaustion and did not know how she would ever walk to the buggy.

Murphy lifted her high into his arms.

She laid her head on his shoulder and closed her eyes. She did not wake when he put her in the carriage or when he carried her to her room when they arrived at Todd's house.

"She'll feel differently when she wakes."

Todd must have seen the coldness in Katie's eyes, Murphy realized. It was as if the love she had for Murphy died out there in the woods. Still, he would not change the events of the day. Katie would heal now and that was the important thing.

However, if she thought to hate him for long she had another thing coming. Whatever the cost, Katie Thomas would find out that he was the man for her. He told Todd, "Let me know when she wakes."

Katie did not wake the rest of the day or night and it was late the next afternoon before she finally went downstairs.

Todd searched for food in the kitchen cabinets. "How do you feel?" he asked carefully.

"Like I need a perfumed bath," she told him. She had been fresh two days before and woke in her clothes that afternoon. She had already picked out a dark skirt and white button-up blouse. They were in the bag at her side.

Todd watched her over the rim of his glasses. "Murphy's replacement came today."

The news stopped Katie in her tracks because she

had turned to walk out of the kitchen. "His replace-ment? That means he will be able to start his ranch."

"That's right. He won't be hanging around our kitchen every morning."

Katie did not like the way Todd said that. No, she definitely did not like it.

Todd rummaged in the cabinet again. "Do you want something to eat before you go? You must be hungry."

Katie started for the front room and called behind her. "I'll eat when I return."

So Murphy's replacement had come and now Katie would find out the sheriff's true intentions. He had said that he did not want her to leave for Chicago, but now that he had his chance to build his dream, would he care where Katie ended up? He had the moneybag and all the facts sorted out—now what would Murphy do?

He'd never said that he loved her. No, he hadn't! What was wrong with him? If he loved her, he should have told her and not left her wondering what his true intentions were . . . She walked fast in agitation. What had he said about that woman, Grace Tidewell? She was beautiful but she wasn't the girl for him. Well, how was a girl supposed to know if she was the one?

Soaking in the tub on the right side of the bathhouse, Katie thought about Murphy again. Of course Murphy loved her. She hadn't fallen in love with the man for nothing. The way he looked at her, teased her, and stood close to her, well, if that wasn't love she did not know what it was.

No, that was attraction.

Murphy loved her because he had done everything to rescue her from Anthony Ricci. He had protected her and saved her from the clutches of evil. He had stayed with her in the courtroom and held her hand and he was there when she remembered that awful moment when she killed Hank Walker. That was love, wasn't it?

No, Murphy had simply performed his duty as sheriff. He was a sworn officer of the law and he had done nothing more than the next man would have done. Right?

Well, why *would* Murphy love her? She'd really done nothing to attract the man. She had not trusted him from the start, she had broken his laws, and she had ignored him and told him she'd bought a ticket for Chicago.

Oh, but how she wished Murphy loved her. She had never known a more wonderful man. He was kind and caring and funny and charming, and had she mentioned wonderful? Would she see him today?

Katie washed her hair vigorously. What had she brought to wear, a simple skirt and blouse? She'd need to change when she returned to Todd's. Out of the tub, she dressed quickly, and at the counter she bought a small bottle of Night Musk. Katie liked it and wondered if Murphy would like it too. She squirted a small amount onto her wrist and then onto the hollow of her throat. Immediately the spot on her neck stung and Katie thought she must have sprayed the mist onto a scratch. She gazed into the mirror hanging by the door near the cash register. Small red bumps surfaced there and Katie asked the attendant, "What's this on my throat?"

Hazel leaned toward her and then straightened. "Dead skin."

Dead skin! She definitely could not have *dead* skin when she saw Murphy later today.

The woman told her, "I have a regular beauty regime that sloughs off dry patches. All you need to do is mix citrus juice, baking powder, salt, and garlic together, and scrub it away."

"Salt and *garlic*?" Katie asked, scratching her wrist.

"Yes, the graininess of the salt scrubs your skin."

Once outside, her throat started to itch. Maybe she would pick up the supplies at the grocers just in case the redness spread. While the clerk filled her order, Barney stepped through the door. Katie hugged him and when she left the shop, he followed her. He asked, "What are all those bumps on your neck?"

"You can see them?"

"Yes, ma'am. They're right there underneath your face."

"Underneath . . . ?" She touched her chin and gasped. The dead skin had multiplied!

In Todd's kitchen, Katie spilled the contents of the bag onto the counter. She had not asked Hazel at what ratio to mix the ingredients so she used half the box of soda, added half a cup of salt, generously sprinkled in crushed garlic, and added a splash of lemon juice. The mixture started to bubble and then the gelatinous globs produced a toxic smell that pushed Katie and Barney backward.

"What *is* that?" Barney howled.

Katie took the bowl outside to the stoop, not noticing how the flowers on the walkway wilted and the jays in the elm tree flew westward to get upwind of the stench.

Barney squatted next to Katie, sitting on his boots and craning his neck to see what Katie would do next. "What's it for?"

"The bumps on my neck," she told him, laying the spoon aside and trying to get up the nerve to reach into the bowl and smear it beneath her jaw.

"You're gonna put that on your *face*?"

Katie frowned at him.

"I thought you meant to make a stinker bomb out of it to chase the chickens out of the garden."

"Do you see a garden out here, Barney?"

"I meant my mother's garden."

Katie scooped a gooey glob with her fingers. "This is a beauty recipe."

Barney cringed in disgust when she smeared some of it onto her neck and jaw.

She did not know how much time to give the solution to work but realized it would not be long after she started to gag and her eyes watered. "Help me to the pump, Barney. I'm struck blind!" She grabbed for his hand and found it. He led her to the side yard and while Katie tried to catch her breath, he jacked the pump furiously.

"Splash your face, Miss Katie," he urged her.

"Lord save me, I can't see the flow." She reached toward the splashing noise and when she leaned the wrong direction, Barney slung the water at her.

Katie raised her hands in self-defense. "Just direct my hands," she told him, spitting water from her mouth.

Barney grabbed her fingers, stuck them beneath the flow, and then pumped the handle wildly.

Able to breath again, Katie peered at the boy through drops clinging to her lashes. "You're not allowed to help me with my beauty treatments ever again."

Barney tried to apologize but was too busy squealing with laughter.

She straightened and squared her shoulders. The front of her blouse was completely soaked. Pushing wet hair out off her face, she flicked the excess water at the boy.

"I thought you said that stuff is supposed to make you beautiful."

Katie narrowed her eyes. "Why do you say that?"

He studied her neck and chin with his brows bunched together. "The red spots are bigger."

Her hands flew to her throat. "You're kidding."

"No, ma'am," he told her, following her into the house.

Katie ran for the mirror in the front room. Large red welts covered her neck and chin. She looked at her wrists that itched as badly. Adding to the hideousness, her hair dripped and matted to the side of her head. "Oh my . . ." She looked at Barney.

He offered a puzzled frown.

Hopeless now, she flopped into the wingback chair and let her hands dangle over the arms of the upholstery. She could not let Murphy see her like this. "What am I going to do?" she asked Barney while trying to stay calm.

He took a seat on the footstool and said, "My mother says powder covers a multitude of imperfections."

"Powder? Do you think powder is going to fix this?"

"Nope."

Katie flopped backward again.

"You might look better if you comb your hair and change you clothes."

"Oh, really? Do you think so?"

"Nope," he said again and stood. "Can I take the rest of that mixture home with me? I'll bring the bowl to you tomorrow."

She regarded him miserably. "Why, are you going to bomb the chickens in the garden?"

"I'm going to bomb the outhouse when Rachel goes inside."

"Who's Rachel?"

"The prettiest girl in Victor City."

Katie frowned at him but he had already walked away. She stood and turned toward the mirror again. Murphy would not bomb any outhouses for her while she looked like this.

The thought depressed her.

Thinking of Murphy, Katie thought she heard his voice. It came from outside the kitchen door. She heard Barney's laughter and suddenly a wave of panic rolled over her. Murphy!

Katie rushed toward the stairs intending to find a tall-collared blouse in her wardrobe.

Todd opened the middle door in the hall just as Katie flew by. When she saw him, she decelerated abruptly and climbed the stairs in a composed manner.

"What's that on your chin?" he called to her. "And what's that awful smell?"

Katie did not answer or even look at him. She went into her room, closed and then locked the door. She wiggled out of the wet skirt and blouse and left them on the floor. Quickly, she rummaged through the wardrobe for one of her winter dresses, thinking to cover her neck and her wrists at the same time. She chose the red one with a high lace collar and pulled it roughly into place. Next, she brushed her hair and studied her reflection. Well, if she didn't look like someone who'd fallen off a potato wagon!

She nearly jumped out of her skin when Todd knocked on the door. "Murphy's downstairs."

Katie groaned and wrung her hands. The welts on her neck itched like crazy. "Tell him I'm not here."

The door handle jiggled. "He knows you're here," Todd said in a clipped tone. "Unlock the door."

"Tell him that I don't feel well," she said, eyeing the window leading to the veranda. She had escaped that way once . . .

"Kathryn Rebeccah, open this door now. The man is waiting for you and I won't have you acting rudely in my house."

How about if Kathryn Rebeccah went outside to act rudely? Unlocking the pin at the sill, she shoved at the window.

"Open the door." It was Murphy's voice this time.

Katie gasped. She tiptoed toward the door but did not open it. "Wade, I don't want to see you right now." She saw the knob turn and then rattle.

His hand thumped hard against the wood and Katie jumped backward.

"Open the door now, Katie. I want to talk to you."

"What about?" she asked, stalling and making her way toward the window.

"I know you think I only cared about finding the moneybag but that isn't true. I wanted to help you get over your nightmares."

She tried to throw her voice. "Well, I thank you for that, Sheriff." She draped her leg over the sill.

The knob rattled violently and then his boot crashed against the wood.

Katie slipped onto the veranda but Murphy caught up to her quickly and spun her around by the elbow. Grabbing both her arms, he dragged her toward him. His eyes looked steely gray and his jaw set. "Why do I have to chase you out windows?" He gave her a small shake. "Why do you think you have to run from me?" His eyes scanned her features. "And what is that all over your neck?"

Katie wanted to cry. She covered her chin with her hands. "I told you that I didn't want to see you!"

Murphy dropped his hands to his hips. "That's why you didn't want to see me?"

She nodded with a tear slipping over her hand.

To her surprise, he laughed. Then his arms came around her and he rested his chin on her damp hair. "I thought you were angry because I took you out to the woods two days ago."

Katie enjoyed the feel of his arms around her. He smelled wonderful, like the wood smoke on the stove where he cooked his awful tasting breakfast. She pressed the palms of her hands to his chest and tried to look at him. "You did care about the money, Wade, you told me you did."

"Not at the expense of losing your love, Katie."

She saw in his expression that he spoke the truth. "You didn't lose my love." She barely got the words out of her mouth before he pressed his lips to hers. His mouth felt warm, exciting, and alive with passion. Katie wrapped her arms around his neck to pull him close, returning his kiss with vigor. When he gazed at her again, she asked, "What if I look like this forever, will you still love me?"

"Look like what?"

"My neck, my wrists . . . I sprayed perfume on them."

"Garlic perfume?"

"No, garlic was the cure."

Murphy frowned at her. "Todd told you to put garlic on a welt?"

"Todd? I didn't ask Todd."

"Of course not. Why would you ask a doctor?"

"Right . . ." She grinned at him. "I hear your replacement is here. That means you'll be leaving town."

"Yes, and so will you."

"I will? Oh, I guess I will, but I missed my stage."

Murphy shook his head. "You would've never got on the stage."

"What makes you so sure?"

"Because I guarded the depot and if you'd stepped one foot inside of it I would have kidnapped you myself."

"I wouldn't have complained if you did."

He seemed very serious then. "Marry me, Katie Thomas."

"I will marry you, Wade Murphy."

He kissed her again and Katie's heart swelled with happiness. She lifted her arms to encircle Murphy's neck and all the misery of the past month disappeared . . . But Katie knew she would do it all over again, all for the love of Murphy.